Fifty Percent
Of Infinity

John A Connor

John A Connor
Fifty Percent of Infinity
This edition published in 2018 by
Chalkway Graphics
Haben
West Sussex
GU31 5HS
The right of John Connor to be identified as
the author of the work has been asserted by him
in accordance with the
Copyright, Design & Patents Act 1988
All rights reserved. No part of this publication
may be produced in any form or by any means -
graphic, electronic or mechanical including
photocopying, recording, taping or information
storage and retrieval systems – without the prior
permission, in writing, of the publisher.
Cover designed by Chalkway Graphics.
Photo courtesy NASA.

Also by John A Connor and available from Amazon Kindle

SPECULATIVE FICTION

Short Circuits

The late **Sir Patrick Moore**, Astronomer and TV Presenter
described **Short Circuits**, John A Connor's first collection of stories as:
*"A very lively and entertaining little book.
When you read it, you will find something to really appeal to you.
I am sure you will enjoy reading it as much as I did."*

Fifty Percent of Infinity

Twenty more, thought provoking tales from the world just around the corner:
a world that may or may not be our own

Seventeen Times as High as the Moon

Everything from alien encounters to temporal displacement; talking fridges
to intergalactic song contests.
Even people who think they don't like science fiction, like this science fiction!

GHOST STORIES

Whines & Spirits

Whines and Spirits was placed in the
Top Five Anthologies for 2015 by noted reviewer Astradaemon's Lair
http://astradaemon.blogspot.co.uk/2015/12/top-five-anthologies-of-
2015.html.

*"What is it that frightens you, when you're alone
in a house that ISN'T haunted?"*
That's the question one of the characters in this collection of stories asks
- just before he finds out how truly frightened you can be in one that is!

HUMOROUS

Puck's Hassle

Take a trip down the sideroads of your imagination and discover that
Jakarta's neckline isn't the only thing going down in the elusive village of
Puck's Hassle.

This one for Ferris

John A Connor was born in Petworth, West Sussex,
attended the old Midhurst Grammar School,
trained in graphic design at
the West Sussex College of Art in Worthing
and went on to a career with the provincial press.
He has had numerous stories and articles published
and was the illustrator of a sci-fi comic strip
which ran for a record-breaking twenty-nine years.

CONTENTS

Strangers in the Night 1
Plant Crossing 5
What Dreams Are Made Of 9
Fifty Percent of Infinity 13
Missing, Presumed Lost 21
Portal 25
Laika 29
Dream, Baby 33
You Have One New Message 41
Affair of the Heart 45
Mistaken Identity 49
End of the Line 63
Living in Realtime 65
Slow Lane 73
End of Term 79
Pick and Mix 95
World's End 99
Information Overload 105
Unquiet Meals 111

Strangers in the Night

It had been an odd day Henderson remembered, afterwards: one of those days that threatens a storm and keeps you waiting a long time for its arrival.

He'd woken after an uncomfortable night, his skin hot and sticky and scarred by the creases in his jumbled bedclothes. Wrapped in a towel, he'd eaten breakfast on the veranda and watched as the clouds gathered low, misshapen and oppressive above the estuary: dirty, grey and purple, like an inverted tray of offal.

By afternoon the heat had forbidden all activity and he had stood in the cool air from the fridge drinking a beer and watching as sharp, white light flickered through the dark overcast and thunder drum-rolled a response.

The evening had brought no relief; the cloud cover had hastened an unseasonable gloom and when he'd stepped from his door, into the stifling air of the garden, the distant sea was already lost to sight and the woods were an indigo stain on the river's folded hillsides. He'd paused, just beyond the cottage's porch, and fumbled for his pipe and lighter and, just as he'd depressed the lever, to strike the flint, the entire landscape from garden to horizon had been illuminated by an explosion of light. The two events had been so nearly simultaneous, the rasping of the steel against the flint and the starkly emblazoned scenery, that for the tiniest moment in time, Henderson had seen them as cause and effect and had been frozen in awe at the spectacle. In that brief instant every item within his view had been captured on his retina like a wildly

Fifty Percent of Infinity

overexposed photograph. The chestnut fence delineating his property, the trees, the curving grass slopes, the flat, silver channel of water widening into the bright, far off mirror of ocean, were all etched into his visual cortex. And so too was the figure of a man standing at the garden's further gate

The intensity of the light had faded almost at once but a soft glow had continued to suffuse the air and there had been a remaining tension and a high, thrumming note, almost outside of human perception. As he'd stood waiting for the after images to fade, Henderson had felt the hair rising and floating from his scalp and, in some manner which he could not have articulated, it had seemed to him that all of nature was waiting for the completion of the lightning's action.

When he had remembered the stranger, glimpsed on the garden's boundary, he'd turned and approached him and, studying him in the curious, half-light, had recognised at once, something familiar about his stance, his build, his faintly lit features. Was it someone from the village? A local he had encountered on a Sunday sojourn to the pub? A footpath ran next to the cottage and walkers often strayed onto the property. It was late in the day but that was the probable explanation for the man's presence. Henderson had been about to make this suggestion when the man had spoken first.

'Looking for the footpath,' he'd said, and the inflection had made it sound more as if he was seeking confirmation than providing explanation.

'Well,' Henderson had responded, noting for the first time that his visitor was also a pipe-smoker, 'it's easy to miss the stile in the hedge.'

'That it is,' had replied the other, 'although Margo insists that it's clear enough, if you're paying attention.'

'Margo?' Henderson's heart had stirred at mention of that name.

Strangers in the Night

'My wife; she'll probably be down in a moment, we usually spend a few minutes taking in the view before dinner.'

'You come here regularly?' Henderson had frowned. If the couple made a habit of enjoying the estuary's panorama they might be expected to know the proper rights-of-way.

'I suppose you could put it that way, certainly every few weeks through the summer. No point in having a holiday home if you don't use it. Have you already met Margo by the way? You seemed to recognise the name.'

'No, no,' Henderson had insisted, 'it's just that I used to know a girl called Margo - a long time ago.'

So, they were weekenders, just as Henderson and that other, lost Margo had planned to become, all those years before, when they had first discovered Redland Cove and had fallen in love with the cottage and with each other.

For a while Henderson and the man had stood silently in the near darkness, as the charged air whined and fizzed and the static lifted the hairs along Henderson's forearms.

'It didn't work out,' he had said, eventually, feeling some impulse to unburden himself. 'My fault; didn't want the commitment; stupid really.' And he had lapsed into silence once more, embarrassed by his admission.

He hadn't returned to the village all those years ago as he had promised Margo he would. He had left her, not quite at the altar but not so far from it. How long she had waited at the cottage he had never learned but she had not replied to his letter with its inane and inarticulate excuses and justifications.

He had not come back until last year, when he'd finally rented the cottage that could have been their home and had begun his descent into a depression in which his surroundings reminded him daily of what might have been.

'I'm sorry to hear that,' the stranger had said, in response to that part of the story which Henderson had vouchsafed and then he had stretched, knocked out his pipe on the gatepost and had looked back, up towards the cottage. As he had done so, the glow from the kitchen window had lit his face and Henderson's eyes had widened in recognition.

'Ah, here comes Margo now, come up and say hello,' said the other Henderson and at that instant the strange interlude ended, for a second the air stilled, the charge drained into the soil and then it was as if someone had taken a hold of the sky's edges and flexed it. The heavens reverberated with the noise. It smashed its way across the land, shook the buildings, echoed along the river valley and on its cue the clouds gave way and the rain deluged across the fields, the estuary and the sea.

The two men stood in the downpour and when one turned to face the other, each of them found himself alone.

Plant Crossing

Mrs Manville put down her trowel and frowned at the plant her weeding had revealed beneath the surrounding foliage. It really was most unusual: fleshy and slightly iridescent, with a plump and waxy central stalk adorned with fat, wedge-shaped appendages. And yet, despite its unprepossessing appearance, Mrs Manville found it oddly fascinating.

Whatever its origins, it certainly wasn't something which she had planted herself, and her husband was far too unadventurous to have selected anything as novel on his infrequent visits to the garden centre. To Brian, gardening was about regimentation and control. He grew his vegetables in straight lines at carefully measured intervals and in varieties handed down through several generations of the Manville dynasty. It was a method which mirrored his approach to life in general, Mrs Manville reflected wistfully, her thirty years with Brian having proved to be every bit as predictable, regulated and carefully managed as his horticulture.

Three days later the strange plant had grown considerably. It had become less translucent, its parts more unified, its shape more distinct.

Mrs Manville had already expended considerable effort on researching its genus with little success. She had not always been Mrs Manville she had reminded herself with determination; as Janet Neville BSc, she had begun a career in biochemistry half a lifetime ago and the visitor to her border had awakened an enthusiasm which she had thought lost forever. Still, she could find nothing helpful in the literature and had come to a sudden decision, which had excited her and alarmed her husband when she had emerged from the loft triumphantly bearing her old microscope.

'For heaven's sake Janet,' he had remonstrated, 'what is the point of going to all that trouble to identify some damned weed?' and then he had rechecked his briefcase, marked his route in coloured, felt-tipped pens on a road atlas and set off for a five-day conference on cost analysis in Harrogate.

Mrs Manville had kissed him dutifully on the cheek and hurried back to the spare bedroom where she had spent an enthralling afternoon studying pieces snipped from the mysterious plant.

By the end of that day she had completed her investigations but was unwilling to admit, even to herself, the consequences that arose from it.

On her next visit to the border she found the plant had grown even more. Its girth had increased almost to match her own, the appendages had developed into ersatz limbs, and yet the roots, which had clearly marked its firm attachment to the soil had atrophied.

Mrs Manville ate a scrappy dinner, her mind elsewhere, then she returned to her room, fed her notes into the shredder, packed her microscope back into its carrying case and returned it to the loft. Then she began a search of the attic, pulling aside bags and suitcases until, with a grunt of confirmation, she hauled a cardboard box over to the hatch and sat, legs dangling above the landing, whilst she turned each find to the light for identification.

Speculative science had been her secret passion as a student but, since her marriage, Brian's disdain for anything so fanciful had embarrassed her into

Plant Crossing

consigning the collection to the cobwebs beneath the rafters.

Now, her examination of the organism developing amongst her shrubbery had reminded her of an idea advanced in the 80s. Yes, here it was, a paper by the British astronomer, Sir Fred Hoyle. He had hypothesised that life existed throughout the universe and was distributed by meteoroids and comets. Panspermia: that's what it was called. Life seeded from space. And it was relevant right now because that "thing" out in the garden was no Earthly plant, her examination had made that clear.

She sat there, on the edge of the loft, and let the thought sift through her consciousness.

Body snatchers: vegetable pods from space that replaced humans with perfectly grown replicas. Triffids: bio-engineered, sentient plants with a lethal aggressive streak. Even, The Little Shop of Horrors, with its man-eating pot plant. If the object of her interest was an alien life form, what would be its motive for setting-up home on our planet? To replace her, devour her? Mrs Manville felt a thrill of fear and excitement play through her body.

Outside, in the gathering dusk, a shadowy, almost-human shape, dragged itself from the soil and moved purposefully towards the unlocked house door.

*

Brian Manville arrived home late having misread his coloured marker pens in the misleading glow of the sodium streetlights. He followed the drive round to the rear of the property, parked on the gravel and, having collected his case and a carrier bag of brochures and conference notes from the boot, made his way across the garden to the kitchen door.

Fifty Percent of Infinity

He paused at the flower border and noted with satisfaction, a wide hole, where the plant, which had caused him such irritation, had once grown. Janet, it seemed, had finally come to her senses and consigned the ugly specimen to the compost heap.

He was vexed by the open door and surprised by the line of smeared prints crossing the tiled floor. His wife was sometimes careless of sensible procedures but she was usually fastidious enough about the home.

He sighed and crossed into the hallway where he paused, his coat raised halfway to the rack, his head to one side. He had heard a noise from above, from the direction of their bedroom. It was a sound with which he was unfamiliar. It was the sound of Janet, giggling.

What Dreams Are Made Of

He sat, hands poised over the keys, eyes fixed on the empty, white screen. It was all very well for the doctor to say, 'write it all down, Harry,' but quite another matter to get the procedure underway. He hadn't really written anything since school - the odd report when he was still working; a stumbling letter of condolence when yet another of his circle of friends or family bit the dust - but none of it was what he thought of as "proper writing", the sort of thing Muriel had done with that group she had attended in the local hall. If she'd still been alive maybe he could have dictated it and let her worry about the construction, the coherence, the presentation of the thing. He sighed and tapped a few, first, tentative words.

Mars isn't the way it looks in the pictures sent back by the NASA rovers. Those always make the terrain look so "limited", the horizons close, the hills low: like a film set, constructed in a confined space. When you are actually there, the scale is altogether different.

Harry paused. *"When you are actually there...?"* He sighed, because that was the whole point, wasn't it? He hadn't been there, and the act of recording it now was an attempt to establish the fictional origins of his dreams; recognise his night-time delusions for what they were.

'It's not incipient dementia,' Doc Cranmer had insisted, when he had told him how his sleeping hours were crammed with visual extravagance and wild mental activity. 'It's not unusual for people of your age to experience an increase in neural stimuli when the body is at rest.'

'But they seem so real!' he had retorted, 'and I remember every minute, too. You don't usually do that with dreams, do you doctor?'

'Generally, no, but full recall isn't as uncommon as people think and in your case, it may be a positive benefit, Harry. I suggest you write up an account of your experiences, every morning, while they are still fresh in your mind. Turn them into a story and you will soon lose your anxiety about them. And don't worry, you aren't going mad, or even mildly deranged, I assure you! A scrap of every news story you ever heard, every cheap paperback you ever read, is lodged somewhere in your temporal cortex and it's from those sources that your midnight mind is constructing these unlikely scenarios. Write them down and learn to love 'em! Who knows, you may end up with the next best seller!'

He had smiled, wanly and promised to give it his best go and now, here he was, on the first paragraph of that award-winning novel.

Standing on the hard, red rocks, and straining your eyes up between the sand-eroded walls of a five-mile high canyon, to a meandering strip of dusty pink sky, the sheer bloody magnificence of the planet takes your breath away...

He was getting into his stride now, the words flowing smoothly from brain to fingers, the text unravelling magically across the open document. That night he dreamed again and in the morning added to his tale.

I've been walking in what I call the "river valley", a mile north from the camp. Of course, there's no water there now, but the clear patterns of its erosion wave

What Dreams Are Made Of

across the fossilised sediment of the streambed, dry for aeons. You can stand on the ancient banks of that river and watch the dust devils rise and fall as they skitter across the wide, gritty desert between here and the mountain ridge, which forms the boundary of this world.

'I sometimes worry that I'm getting too immersed in the story.' He watched, with mild concern as the doctor studied the printouts from the previous week's work. 'I mean, I spend the night experiencing events "live" as it were, and then most of the morning reliving them in print. Is that healthy?'

'I don't think you've any need to worry, and look - this is terrific stuff you know! More like a travelogue than a novel perhaps, but I'm sure its relieving the stress you were feeling before. I've no doubt the best course is to continue your writing and, in time, the dreams will dissipate and you'll wake refreshed and clear headed.'

'I hope you're right doctor. Sometimes Mars seems more real to me than Earth.'

Harry felt tired and distracted after his visit to the surgery. In a desultory frame of mind, he shopped for food, trailing down the supermarket's aisles, staring listlessly at the shelves of incomprehensibly marked packets and cans. He called in at The Fountain and drank a solitary pint before walking home through the deserted park. The house was cold and empty and he turned up the central heating, threw himself down on the sofa and fell into a fitful sleep.

When he awoke it was already dark outside; he closed the blinds and, passing the desk in the corner of the room, reached down and switched on the computer. When the screen lit he eased down into the vacant chair and ran his fingers over the keyboard.

Fifty Percent of Infinity

Once more my night was disturbed and chaotic, my mind crowded with all manner of strange ideas and concepts. I found myself on the Earth, in a strange town, searching the shelves of a store for packaged food; wandering the corridors between freezer cabinets and racks of newly baked bread. In a nearby tavern I purchased a glass of cold beer and then walked aimlessly past ornamental ponds and dark, green shrubbery - all the while the sky fading from a clear, icy blue to a deep indigo, studded with stars. And, when I woke, I remembered all these things with the utmost clarity and, so, as the doctor has advised, I am setting them down in the hope that this will free my mind from future disturbance.

Harry rose, stumbled into the recycler and let the thin stream of tepid water sting him into wakefulness. Outside his unit's Plexiglas dome the Martian sunrise was already fringing the mountains with a pale, yellow light. It was time for his appointment with the station's robodoc and he waved a hand across the sensor to activate the holographic link.

'How's it going?' asked the android.

'Same old dreams every night,' answered Harry.

'Still finding yourself on planet Earth?'

'As ever - and so vivid I remember every minute. As you advised, I'm dictating the whole thing to an autoscribe soon as I wake. Do you really think it'll do any good?'

'I'm sure of it,' replied the bio-botic medic. 'The therapy will rid your mind of these delusions and re-establish your hold on reality. Turn your dreams into a story and you will soon lose your anxiety about them.'

Harry frowned as he deactivated the transmission.

The doc's parting remark had left him with the oddest feeling of déjà vu.

Fifty Percent of Infinity

I died on a Thursday. Everyone at the laboratory knew I'd died, a good part of my brain having been spread across the white board, obliterating, in the process, the scrawled formula that might otherwise have led them to an explanation for the accident. And yet, death wasn't quite what ensued, when I threw the switch and activated the world's first and most spectacularly successful, personality download.

'What's half of infinity, Dad,' asked Simon, as his father crossed the kitchen, en route to the back door and, ultimately, The Dog and Partridge, saloon bar.

'Yer what?' asked his father in return, playing, pointlessly, for time, in a game for which he had not even been dealt a hand, leave alone had time to arrange the cards.

'Infinity, what's fifty percent of it? Do y'know, Dad?'

It was amazing the way in which the boy could maintain that air of genuine enquiry; hold his features like that - eyebrows part-raised, head inclined questioningly, not a trace of derision creasing the corners of his mouth. Waiting for the moment of admission, when he would look down at his books, but not allow the action to hide his smirk.

'Infinity? That's, like "never ending" int it?'

Fool to prevaricate, better by far to admit ignorance.

Fifty Percent of Infinity

'Yeah, that's right, Dad. What d'ya reckon happens when you divide it by two?'

'Dunno.' His voice was barely audible, his head bowed.

'Don'tja Dad? Don'tja know, eh? Think about it Dad, go on.'

'Look, Simon, I don't know about things like that, d'y'see? And, I've gotta get off t' darts match. Don't wanna be late.'

As he hurried through the door, into the unlit porch, he could feel the contempt radiating from the fourteen-year-old at the kitchen table.

The little brat! But surely, there was something to admire in his desire to break free from the stupefying banality of life on the Cricklefield Estate, the unedifying example of his shallow mother. If ever you needed confirmation that beauty was just skin-deep Gloria Hudderstone certainly provided it. Underneath the lip-gloss pout and the page-three-figure, she was a self-centred little cow and her son could hardly be blamed for inheriting her callous nature.

As for her other half, the poor, simple sod who'd provided legitimacy for the product of her promiscuous behaviour, well, the boy had soon identified the intellectual gulf that lay between them and had responded accordingly. The calculated way in which he made sure to always called him "Dad", just to emphasise the obvious lack of any such familial tie; two fingers in the air to his surrogate parent.

Half of infinity, ha! Don'tja know, Dad? Don'tja? My God the pretensions of youth, eh?

Infinity. Now, there's a thing: The state or quality of being infinite. Anaximander - he thought he knew, two-and-a-half thousand years ago. Euclid, Archimedes - they'd had a go at a definition too. Bruno proposed an "unbounded" universe:

Fifty Percent of Infinity

"innumerable suns, innumerable planets" and, if the universe does indeed have a flat topography, as recent analysis of radiation patterns seem to suggest, then the cosmos really is infinite ...

'Hello, Ted, on yer way t' darts match? I've had me dinner and me arrows are in me pocket, lad, so we's all ready to see off Red Lion, eh?'

It was Pete Stansley from the estate.

'Hello Pete, aye, reckon as I'm bound fer the same bar as you. Think we kin take buggers tonight?'

'You just keep throwing like last Thursday and trophy's good as won, Ted. And don't worry 'bout scoring - I'll keep tally and shout out what y' need. You just heed to me lad and we're home and dry - well, mebbe not so dry here's hoping, eh?'

'That's good of you Pete, you know I'm nay so quick with the numbers and all.'

'Well, you just concentrate on hitting them doubles, lad, that's all that matters.'

He nodded, thoughtfully and fell into step with his team-mate.

Since the accident, that had been all that mattered: hitting the doubles; finding those small moments of achievement. Although to begin with, of course, there'd been long periods of confusion and disorientation.

The pub was already full when they pushed their way inside, members of both teams busy divesting themselves of coats and scarves, ordering drinks, making introductions. On the far side of the room, darts were already thudding into the board as others made good use of their earlier arrival to put in a little pre-match practice.

Ted smiled quietly and nodded in the direction of one or two familiar faces as he hung his coat and reached into a side pocket for the hard, plastic box that contained his newly flighted darts.

'Still goin' wi' feathers, I see Ted.' It was Geoffrey, team captain.

'Oh, aye, still the feathers.' Ted didn't look up, just removed the darts, replaced the lid and returned the box to his pocket. 'Seem t' work fer me.'

'Let's hope they do - yer on first, gi' it yer best, lad.'

Ted smiled again, moved to the mat, waited patiently for the assembly to organise itself, his opponent to appear, drinks to be carried to window-sills, positions to be taken around the board; waited for the signal, to begin.

For some time, I believed I'd survived the blast when the torus exploded. After all, I seemed to be in one piece, albeit that I appeared to have been thrown clear through the lab window and into the well-kept flowerbeds which Alpha Pioneering maintained to impress visiting dignitaries. I was sitting, dazed, among the broken tulips, staring back into the confusion of smoke and flame and trying to make sense of what had happened. It was when I hauled myself to my feet and hurried unsteadily across to the wreckage that I had my first indication that something very odd had occurred.

'One hundred and forty!' Geoffrey bellowed to make himself heard over the din of convivial conversation and shouted encouragement. Ted took a long stride towards the tyre-framed board, reached out and extracted his three darts in quick succession. As he turned to the side to clear the throwing area, the captain's big hand grasped his shoulder for a moment. 'Well done, lad, great start. Keep it up, eh?'

That action, of pulling myself up from among the bruised and flattened flowers, had taken place without the proper intervention of my brain. That is, the decision to rise had not been my own. Hands had been thrust down into the crumbling soil, muscles braced, the body's centre of gravity shifted and the legs flexed to push it erect but I had not instigated any of those movements.

I guessed I was in shock or suffering concussion, my sensory inputs temporarily numbed, my movements impelled by some kind of instinctive reaction. Then I stepped through the breach in the laboratory wall and looked down on my dismembered body and I began to understand the truth.

'One hundred!' As Ted retrieved his darts for the second time a chorus of approval rose up around him.

'Great stuff, Ted,' it was Pete, pushing a pint glass into his hand. 'Yer done and dusted on this one I reckon! Just a double top, a...'

'One and a double ten,' finished Ted, taking a pull of his bitter.

'Aye...that's right, good lad...aye.' Pete appraised his friend, curiously. 'You enrolled in Open University Ted! That it?'

'No, no, I just...' his voice trailed off into silence and he covered his confusion with another mouthful of beer.

'Nay, don't fuss yersel', lad! I always said as it would rub off on y' eventually, din't I? Go on, get in there and wind it up!'

There was an irony in my situation. Ted had been weeding just a few feet away, beyond the open window, when I threw the switch that changed both our lives forever. In the microsecond following the plasma chamber's destruction, my entire

Fifty Percent of Infinity

consciousness, the imbedded electronic patterns and impulses which constituted what I thought of as "myself", were torn free and transmitted to the nearest receptors, the synaptic pathways of the gardener's cerebrum.

My intention had been to copy my entire personality, every electrical impulse, the switching of each relay, the totality of my recorded memory - conscious and sub conscious - and download it into electronic storage. The meltdown had closed that route and, at the same time, created, just for an instant, some kind of charged environment which had snatched away the signal and embedded it into that other brain.

I was now, I supposed, only a duplication of my original self. He, had indeed, died in that fiery detonation.

Ted's next throw caught the wire on the twenty's edge and turned the dart into the adjacent "One". A descending sigh echoed around the bar.

'Ted, y' need...'

'I know, Pete. Twenty and a double-top.' Ted shifted his stance, took aim on the second dart.

That's twice he's seen the sequence he needs to close out the game. There was a time, when he couldn't subtract beyond the fingers of one hand! It's my influence I'm sure, but it's the extent to which I have any effect on his, oh so mundane, life. It's been a dozen years now and I remain dormant in a corner of his mind. Along for the ride; seeing what he sees, feeling what he feels but having only a miniscule influence on his actions and no contact with him on a conscious level. A prisoner with an IQ of 155 chained within a mind barely above that of a mental retard.

And the irony? There was a time once before, when the thin wall of my laboratory had been all that separated me from one of the low-paid, menials who grubbed for a living in the gardens and kitchens of Alpha Pioneering.

I had looked up one day to see her, peering through the glass, palms resting on the bar of her trolley, the handles of her mops and brooms criss-crossed, tepee like against the sun. She was young and beautiful and I felt a sudden flush of desire for her. I'd been working hard for months, given no thought to such matters, but all at once I knew I must have her.

There was no difficulty in gratifying my lust; she responded at once to my encouragements, led on by her own sexual appetites and a wide-eyed naiveté, which I was only too willing to exploit. For a while I satisfied myself with her company and then one afternoon she told she was pregnant. The little fool! For a while she seemed to expect that I would share responsibility for the state she had carelessly imposed upon herself but then, seeing the impossibility of such a demand, she sought out another's protective embrace.

Ted smiled once more for the photograph. The trophy rested on the low table around which the team were seated; he had played his part in its winning and that, and three pints of bitter, had left him happy and content, only the thought of his return home troubling his mind.

He had loved Gloria since his days in primary, although he had understood even then that her beauty was reserved for others, his awkward ways and slow mind, an obstacle that would always lie between them. The reality was still, after all these years, something hard to comprehend. She waited for him now, in his home, in his bed, and a part of his mind gave thanks that such a thing could be so. And although she did not love him, he hoped that one day she might.

Fifty Percent of Infinity

Her child though, was beyond his comprehension: both clever and cruel, she said that his father had died, that day in the complex, and would otherwise have married her, but Ted was not sure that could be true. What he did know was that there would never be understanding between him and the boy and he grieved for that loss and the parent his son might have had.

Soon now, we will turn for home, unsteady footsteps down the crooked street. The girl has made him a man; even maybe, learned to love him, in her way. The accident has brought him his greatest desire and found her a kind of limited contentment I suppose and he asks no questions when she dresses up and leaves the house; knowing she'll return is all that he can ask. As for me, I watch their world through his eyes and share his lifetime and the family I shunned, and every second is a year and every year an infinity.

Infinity is an abstract concept and, as such, has no numerical value. Halve infinity and the concept is still infinite.

Missing, Presumed Lost

We learned everything, little by little, year by year, because in that way, Gabriel said, the day would come when we would know everything there was to know. I wasn't sure about that. I had a feeling that even old Granddad Cole didn't know all there was to know about the world and he was over ninety years old. Still, Gabriel was a mighty keen teacher and, as time went by, something of what he told us tunnelled its way into our heads and found a home there.

By the time I was ten or so I understood that the world was flat and that the sea poured off the edges all around, like water from a bucket under a dripping pump. I knew too that the wind blew the sea back into the air so that it fell as rain and that the sun went under the Earth at night to keep the ground warm.

Gabriel said that it was all the work of the Almighty but one time when the moon was high and the cabin door was locked and barred against the night prowlers, Granddad Cole told me the truth. He said there was one thing for sure: not only was the world not run by God it wasn't run by The Devil neither. Those two, he said, had left us to get on with things the best we could and up until now we hadn't made much of a fist of it.

'The future's not written in the stars, young Zekiel,' he told me, as the storm howled around the fire stack and the prowlers answered likewise. 'Nobody knows where we're heading and don't you believe those who say they do. Your path's not mapped out ahead like a man following the riverbed seaward. Tomorrow has no

Fifty Percent of Infinity

shape until you take it into your hands and squeeze it a little.'

Back then I didn't have a notion what he meant and his heresy scared me more than a mite. I knew that the village tolerated old Cole on account of his age but I sensed, even then, that their indulgence had its limits and wasn't likely to extend to camp followers like myself.

The event which had shaped our lives had occurred way back before Granddad had been born; 'just in time,' he told me, 'to save us from our own greed and avarice,' but when he said that he scowled and spat into the fire.

'Anyway,' he added, 'one day everything changed,' and when I frowned at that, he stared down at his big hands resting on his lap and was silent for so long that I thought he had forgotten our conversation.

'A long while ago,' he continued at last, 'the world was full of wonders and magic. The air sung with words and music and men could fly.'

I must have shown my incredulity because he glowered at me then and lapsed back into silence for a moment or two before suddenly repeating insistently, 'Yes, they could fly and they could conjure up pictures of distant lands with the touch of a finger and speak to each other across the Earth with no more than a whisper.'

I stared, wide-eyed into his dark, furrowed face, not knowing whether to believe or dismiss his wild tales. I knew, of course, that the ancestors had been wise and clever beyond our knowledge. When my friends and I played among the forest trees and underbrush we sometimes traced the fragments of their wide, black track ways, winding away across the hillsides and once, deep in a man-made cave, its once smooth walls cracked and broken by roots and brambles, its further recesses blocked by rock fall, we had discovered a litter of rusting shapes; wheeled vehicles maybe from a time beyond memory.

And the travellers who traded medicine and supplies claimed that these roads crossed great bridges of cast stone and would take you, should you be foolish enough to follow them, on to ruined cities, draped with creeper and vine and filled with the debris of strange devices the purpose of which no one living could determine. And so, maybe Granddad Cole's stories were true and once, the human race had indeed conquered the skies and, for all we knew, reached for the moon.

There came a day, he said, when the magic ceased to work. The carrier waves died, the energy would no longer flow, wires cooled, lights faded. Some natural force had been destroyed and its absence left us stranded, like a beached whale. That's what my grandfather said,' Granddad Cole told me, 'though I can't expect you to understand his words. I can only tell you that he cried when he remembered what was lost.'

'And after that?' I wondered.

'After that the Earth went on turning,' replied Granddad. 'People went on living...and dying, and the world seemed to shrink, day by day. Now we have the age of the Followers of the New Earth. Those fools who claim it was an unnatural knowledge of God's purpose that had led us near to Armageddon. Once there were bonfires clear across the globe as the books were burned,' and he bowed his head and studied his hands once more, before concluding, almost in a whisper, 'and they weren't all that went into the flames, either.'

'But what started it?' I persisted, 'why did the magic disappear?'

'I will tell you what my father told me,' answered old Cole, 'but first know this Zekiel - that world is not lost!' and his eyes blazed with a sudden passion as he grasped me by the shoulders so firmly that I was fixed to the spot.

'The knowledge of centuries lives on and you must take up the torch which will light mankind's way back to understanding and enlightenment. I have devoted my life to the salvation of scientific study and now you must do the same! I have forbidden books, which will guide you away from Gabriel's myths and superstitions. Together you and I can take man back to the stars!'

I shook myself free of his hold and recoiled in horror from his outburst. Scientific study? Forbidden books? 'You will have us arrested!' I cried, in alarm.

'Not if we are careful,' he replied. 'We are not alone; there are others who seek the same goals. With care we can recover all that was destroyed.'

'But why me?' I wailed, 'why is it my destiny to leave the true and proper path?' and I made the sign of The Tree as Followers of the New Earth were taught, to ward off thoughts of scientific heresy.

'Two hundred years ago, said Granddad Cole, 'your great, great, great grandfather helped to build a giant machine, one which could tear apart the fabric of life and reveal the way that God had created matter. One day, the machine ran out of control and the world changed forever. The device was buried deep in the ground, beyond the sea, in a place named CERN - and the old world died there in retribution for their actions. Now you and I must vindicate their work, restore the family's good name and set off on a new quest for the elusive boson!

Portal

Austin sat back from the hood, screwed his eyes shut for a second and then attempted to refocus on the paperwork strewn across his desk. It always took a while to adjust and, each time hunger or fatigue required him to pause in his examination of the target, he found himself a tad more reluctant to resurface, and more mentally and physically drained when he did.

They called it "star stress", the other members of the telescope's small community, and Doctor Millbank, the team's occasional medic, had warned Austin that his particularly extended periods of observation could lead to depression or even mild paranoia.

'It's the scale of the thing that's the problem,' he had observed, during a chance encounter, which Austin suspected to have been engineered by Crosby, the head of the "Habitable Planet Programme".

'Space is big! and the human mind has trouble grasping the concept,' he had continued solicitously. 'Oh, you think you understand - and intellectually, you do; you understand the maths, you can argue the theoretical construct, but the reality is that the human mind simply hasn't evolved to comprehend the true scale of the universe and when it hovers on the edge of such comprehension, the sudden awareness of its own insignificance puts it in peril of overload and breakdown.'

'If you're telling me that the universe can blow your mind, it's a prerequisite of membership around here, Doc,' Austin had responded, lightly.

Fifty Percent of Infinity

He smiled as he recalled the conversation and then stood, stretched and made his way down the access stairway to the mirror housing.

He had been coming here more often, since his anxiety had taken root, and peering through the angled struts that supported the huge parabolic dish.

Its impossible surface gleamed like perfect, white ice, each molecule in continuous, synchronous movement, as the mainframe fought to compensate for aberrations in the Earth's atmosphere and for tiny, seismic ground movements, far beyond any human discernment.

The Mayans, he had read, believed mirrors to be windows into the spirit world, placing polished obsidian discs on their altars and around their dead, to allow for communion between the two states of being. It seemed appropriate that twenty first century man's attempts to uncover life elsewhere in the firmament should use similar, if rather more technically advanced, implements.

He stared out across the unblemished, quasi-metal dish, his mind racing with the possibilities of the mission's success.

They had locked onto a star in a region of space known as Frio368m. Perturbations in its orbit had suggested circling planets a decade earlier but resolution had been too low then, data too limited to determine numbers or size. Now, the mirror that spread before him, had revealed both these facts and had isolated a prime candidate, plumb in the middle of the CHZ, the circumstellar habitable zone or, as the popularisers would have it, the "Goldilocks Zone": that distance from the parent star that provided conditions that were "just right" for habitation by life forms similar to our own.

Austin had spent many hours, staring at that distant point of light, the gathered photons unscrambled and re-presented by systems of a complexity so great that the Mayans would have seen their writers as gods, even though, Austin considered, they were both, the Mexican ancients and the telescope's crew, on the same side of the mirror.

Back at the viewport he cranked the chair into position and pulled the hood down. The image wavered and steadied as the computer modified the optics.

Crosby had named the planet, "Seeker" because, he had explained obliquely, in a sing-song voice, 'we'll have a world of our own'; then he had roared with laughter at Austin's blank expression and refused to expand on the reference.

Seeker was a fuzzy point of light appended to a larger disc, which was the position of the masked sun. Austin gazed out across fourteen light years of space and wondered at the enormity of the occasion. It was not, as the Doctor had suggested, a feeling of his own insignificance which coursed through his body but something altogether different. The possibility of confirming the existence of intelligent life elsewhere in the universe gave him a sense of huge importance, of being a part of something vast and awe-inspiring. The anxiety arose from the desperate need to advance that state.

He knew that what he observed was not the planet itself but only the mirror's image of the planet, and he had stood, at home, and studied through his own mirror, the reflection of his room, noting the perfection of its reversed world and its three-dimensional integrity. After a while, the mirror world seemed the only reality; when he turned, his living room appeared flat and drab.

So it was with the telescope. He stole every available moment to view Seeker and emerged, when he must, washed out and numb. The mirror was a portal, the light years compressed by its magic qualities. He had begun, he knew, to comprehend a state of being which science had ignored, or failed to comprehend; quantum mechanics at the macro scale.

It was an idea with which Crosby had refused to engage and with his sanity questioned, Austin had known his time was short.

Tonight, he was alone in the dome and this was to be his last visit. Rising from his seat he stepped once more towards the door and out onto the spiral walkway.

He found himself grasping the cold steel framework, finding footholds among the diagonal braces. Above him the dark sky was studied with tiny crystal sparks; below his feet, the broad, silver pool of light engulfed the whole of existence. At its centre, clear and precise, his mind placed the planet, mankind's first step in a future among the stars. With a smile of completion Austin released his grip and fell forward, diving straight and true to the centre of the light and his new beginning.

Laika

BBC News, Sunday, November 10, 1958: Soviet authorities report that Laika, the first dog in space, has died painlessly after a week in orbit although some sources claim that the animal succumbed to over-heating and panic within a few hours of take-off on November 3.

The Quaade eased its form into the position required for neural integration and cast a filigree of nerve tissue across the small, grey organ under examination. It had found the creature close to termination aboard a tiny vessel in orbit about the blue green planet and, because its purpose was always benign, it had brought it aboard and left its transport to circle on alone.

The orbiter's technology had been simple and, to begin with, the Quaade had assumed the diminutive life form to be both designer and pilot, but the lack of manipulative appendages and, on further examination, the configuration of the biological structures that controlled the body, had led it to understand otherwise.

The Quaade's motivation had been rescue rather than research but resuscitation necessitated investigation and it was for this purpose that The Quaade had eased sensory fibres into the unconscious body, whilst remaining incurious as to why a superior intelligence might submit a subordinate one to lonely death far from the planet's surface.

Searching the feebly firing cortex, The Quaade found responses deeply imprinted onto the subconscious: responses once triggered by the craft from which its body had been freed. It sensed too, an all-encompassing trust and a tenuous understanding of that trust's betrayal; then it withdrew, allowing the biological repair systems to assume control.

Cruelty and indifference were only concepts to The Quaade; it knew of them but did not comprehend them. That is to say, it accepted that many primitive life forms could be callous and uncaring and driven to acts of savagery and heartlessness by their genetic and evolutionary history but it was unable to rationalise, even in the abstract, such behaviour. Since the same inherited flaws gave rise to both war and petty spitefulness, The Quaade considered those two outcomes to be equally wretched but, knowing only forbearance, it had no capacity for blame or retribution.

Without its intervention, the failure of the cooling system aboard the simple spacecraft would have led to death by hyperthermia but, even regardless of such malfunction, the craft was clearly incapable of re-entry into the planetary atmosphere and the payload had been condemned from the outset. The Quaade, however, gave no consideration to the sentient beings responsible for this state of affairs, being wholly concerned with the recovery and survival of their victim.

Fluids pumped, nutrients flowed. Slowly life processes returned to optimal. After the planet had turned three times below them, the autonomous repair programme pronounced itself satisfied and the quadruped, which on its home world was known as "dog", was delivered into the presence of The Quaade.

The Quaade in order to accommodate an expected lack of sophistication in the animal's perceptions had reconfigured itself into an upright, four-limbed shape, which approximated to that of the planet's primary, carbon-based, inhabitants.

Laika

The dog approached warily, all four of its appendages working in sequence, the extension holding the brain and sensory organs, low to the ground. The Quaade held its shape and position; the dog sampled the air, intermittently, with a sound like gas escaping a loose valve. Carefully, The Quaade exuded smaller, multiple extensions from an upper limb, intent on mimicking the grasping elements of the species it sought to copy. The dog raised the brain case, repeated the air-sampling action and pushed its tapered, forward-facing end gently into The Quaade's proffered embrace. The Quaade, on impulse, lowered its second pseudopod and ruffled the fur behind the creature's auditory extensions.

BBC News, 14 April 1958: The capsule containing the body of Laika, the first dog in space, burned up in the Earth's atmosphere over Barbados today, five months after launch.

Time is, of course, relative, its passage not easily marked in the absence of planetary motion. Perhaps it can be observed in the emission of radiation from an atom, or maybe in the beating of a heart. By the latter measure a lifetime can be counted out when all else appears unchanged.

The Quaade moved back and considered its work. Here in the central disc of the galaxy the sky was ablaze with stars and there was no atmosphere on this world to scatter the light of the system's distant sun and obscure the awesome view of the cosmos. It seemed a fitting place.

The laser-etched stone bore a few words in The Quaade's own tongue - or at least, that of its remote ancestors, The Quaade itself having long since dispensed with the need for writing. They recorded the brief life of the entity whose name it knew only as a cipher, copied from a protective harness ripped from a burning machine. The Quaade's action had saved that life and its technology had extended its existence to aeons beyond its natural span. By now, the blue, green planet that had been its home would be a cinder, engulfed by its expanding sun and subject to its own heat death; and although irony was a notion incomprehensible to The Quaade, it drew a comparison between the intended fate of the dog and the eventual lot of its masters, and saw a symmetry there.

Even for The Quaade, a being as near immortal as any the universe had spawned, that event above the blue green planet was almost beyond memory and the creature it had rescued, dead five billion years. But death, like time, was a relative state to The Quaade, the processes that cloned and duplicated life, elementary biology. It had raised a marker stone on a hundred million worlds and although the once solitary traveller was still puzzled each time by its sense of loss, it was comforted too by the continuity of its relationship.

The Quaade turned back and waited while it was engulfed by the translucent walls of the self-replicating life form which provided its home and transport. Once within the cavernous interior The Quaade assumed the nearest thing its body knew to a squat and, forming the necessary air bladder, orifice and resonance chamber, whistled for its best friend.

Dream, Baby

'And is that all it does, help you remember your dreams?' Jamie leaned back and regarded his brother with a jaundiced eye. Bio-chemistry was, of course, a more glamorous profession than graphic design, as any number of girls would have testified, had they been called upon to choose between the two, but geekdom ran a very poor third and those same girls would have found it difficult to deny, after time for introspection, that Harry was indeed, a first-class, gold-plated geek.

'All it does?' Harry repeated indignantly, thumping his ginger-beer shandy down so firmly that the liquid scaled the sides of the glass and flooded the table-top. 'All! I don't think you grasp the import of this discovery, Jamie. We're talking total recall here, not just vague recollection. 'Look,' he gathered a handful of beer mats and used their edges to soak up the spill, 'it used to be thought that dreams were insubstantial things, made up from stray memories and fleeting experiences that the subconscious mind cleared away while you slept. But recently we've begun to understand that they are, in fact, the product of the mind's activities as it files away everything of which it's become aware during the last waking period. And I mean, everything!' He paused for effect and found it wanting on his brother's face.

'You still don't get it, do you?' he placed the now saturated mats in a soggy stack on the pub's tiled floor and tried again.

'What do you remember about your last dream? Anything?'

Fifty Percent of Infinity

'I don't often dream,' replied Jamie, 'and when I do, well, you know what it's like, it all fades as soon as you open your eyes. I suppose you could try writing it down straight away...you might hang onto the memory long enough to do that, I dunno. It depends how vivid it is doesn't it? I had a dream the other night where I was at a party with Alex and Shirley and that stuck in my mind.'

'And what were you doing, at this party?'

'I don't know! Just chatting I think, nothing special.'

'What colour socks was Alex wearing?'

'What colour...! Now you're just being ridiculous.'

'Not at all,' Harry smiled knowingly and took a sip of what remained of his beer. 'Your subconscious will have built that dream from actual observations made during the preceding day and what we now know is that the eye and brain register far, far more detail than they allow your conscious mind to access. That picture of Alex, at the party, will have been built from real-time encounters during which, without being fully aware of it, you will have noted, not only the colour of his socks, but the pattern of his tie, the weave of his suit, a stray thread on a loose button - everything about his appearance.'

'But what the hell for?' Jamie spread his hands in an expression of bewilderment. 'I mean, Jesus, why do I need all that useless information?'

'Maybe you don't, and that's why your brain keeps most of it from you, to protect you from overload; but it's all recorded just the same, in case it might be useful, and it's the process of sorting it all out and dispensing with the rubbish that gives rise to your dreams.'

Jamie frowned, gathered up the two now empty glasses and pushed himself up from his chair. 'I'll get another round in,' he said, his mind still distracted by the conversation.

Dream, Baby

When he returned, a few minutes later he had more questions and he posed one of them as he set the beers down and scavenged two new beer mats from an adjacent table.

'You started this off by telling me you'd concocted a drug which enabled you to remember your dreams, right?' Harry nodded in affirmation. 'And then you said that I didn't realise how important that was, OK? But I'm finding it difficult to see how recalling the shade of someone's socks at an imaginary party can be all that vital to life, the universe and what I'm having for dinner.'

'It isn't, it's just an illustration of the complexity and comprehensiveness of the mental interpretation of our sensory input.'

'Ye gods, Harry, do you use that as a chat-up line? So, why is it important?'

'Because, brother dear, it isn't just your friend's taste in clothing that your brain is re-examining in the dark reaches of the night and it's not only information obtained by visual input.'

'Meaning, please Harry.'

'Meaning the information gleaned from your other four senses is every bit as expansive and that it too is examined, minutely, by your grey matter and contributes to your dreams.'

'Still wondering why it's important Harry.'

'I'm coming to that, be patient. The point is that material from all these sources produces an emotional response that is, itself, suppressed to avoid placing the conscious mind under too much stress. So...'

'Hang on, let me play something past you to see if I've got the gist of what you're saying. I meet an attractive girl, for instance...'

'Do you have to translate everything in terms of your libido, Jamie? Yes, I suppose you do, carry on.'

'I meet an attractive girl and the sound of her voice, the smell of her perfume, the feel of her skin, the taste of her lips on mine - stop making that face Harry and concentrate - all of those things turn me on and that effect is controlled by my brain?'

'Well, in your case, I'd say barely, but yes, that's pretty much the way it works. Let's say that your natural animal lust is held in check and instead of your hormones taking control you ask her politely if she'd like to go to the dance on Friday night.'

'You're older than me Harry, that might have worked for you, if you'd ever got around to trying it.'

'Whatever. Now the significant thing is this: the real state of your feelings, the nature of your obsession, if that's what it is, is made clear to your subconscious as it works away, defragging and filing overnight, and it's the temporary spillage from that, that is your dream.'

'Euk! You might like to rephrase that Harry. So, where are you going with this, eh?'

'This is where I'm going, young sibling: total recall will give us access to everything that has hitherto been kept from us. For the first time in the history of mankind, we will fully understand our subconscious minds, our repressed desires, our hidden potential! It will free us from an evolutionary backwater designed to ensure a safe stagnation and allow us to expand and develop into a new race of Homo Mentalis Superioris!'

'Wow!' Jamie pulled in his chin and looked across the table, eyes wide, brows raised. 'You got plans for global domination? Seriously,' he added, spotting signs of extreme annoyance building in his brother's demeanour, 'what are you planning to do with this, "wonder drug"?'

'Test it on myself, of course. All this is conjecture thus far - based on sound scientific research of course. I was brought a new species of epiphytic orchid from which I managed to distil a chemical reagent with very

Dream, Baby

unusual properties. I've identified receptors on the brain that respond, as I predicted, in laboratory primates. Later this week I intend to ingest the drug and record the results. Global domination? No, but I expect my new clarity of mind to bring global recognition and who can say where that might lead? One day, Jamie, you may feel privileged to have been one of the first to learn about this new future for the human race.'

'Can I have your autograph?' asked Jamie, grinning broadly, to detract from the sarcasm. 'Tell you what, I'll give you a call next Monday, and we can meet up to have a chat about how it all went, yeah?'

Harry rolled his eyes to the ceiling and indicated his agreement, with a nod.

***

As things turned out Jamie's call was rendered unnecessary by a text message he received from Harry on Sunday night, suggesting a meeting the following evening at The Smoking Joint, Jazz Cellar. A text from his brother was odd in itself, since communication between them had hitherto been instigated exclusively by Jamie, but an invitation to meet in that particular establishment was extraordinary, given the bar's and Harry's diametrically opposed views of a respectable lifestyle. So, it was with some misgivings that Jamie groped his way down the worn, brick stairway and stepped out uncertainly into the dimly lit fug of The Joint's basement home.

In one corner a band played languidly, in another a couple embraced with an enthusiasm that belied the tempo of the music. A handful of others watched both performances from a line of bar stools or, almost invisibly, from the cellar's shadowed recesses.

Fifty Percent of Infinity

Jamie peered around. Unsurprisingly, there was no sign of his parent's eldest boy. Then, as he hesitated between a swift half and early departure, one of the two entwined figures disentangled its limbs and half-rose to face the bar.

'Jamie! Hey man! How's it going down? Come over and meet Corinth and pick up a drink on the way. Mine's a Dirty Shirley, heavy on the vodka and stick them both on my tab.'

'Harry? HARRY?' Jamie took a step towards the table and squinted into the gloom. Ye gods and little fishes! It couldn't be...it was! Harry! 'Wha...wha...whatta you doing here...with...Corinth?' he spluttered.

'Whaddas it look like bro'?' Harry grinned back, 'want summa the action?'

Jamie forced his feet to carry his body forward and he lowered himself into the chair opposite the pair. Now he looked more closely his certainty about the identification wavered. Shades? Who the hell would wear shades in the sepulchral confines of The Smoking Joint? And those were jeans! Worn, frayed, filthy, yes, all those things, but jeans, never the less. Harry had never worn jeans in his life, his preferred casuals were cavalry twill, with a green and red check shirt not, definitely not, a tie-dyed sleeveless granddad vest adorned with a string of vaguely African beads.

Jamie leaned across the table and lifted the glasses free; the eyes beneath actually squinted against the twenty-five-watt glare of the bar-room but there was no doubt, they belonged to his big brother; he dropped them back into place and reclined with a sigh.

'Tell me,' he instructed, 'what happened after you swallowed that rain-forest goo?'

'No swallowing man, it was all done intravenously.' Harry gestured to the bartender who, in view of Jamie's indisposition, had decided to deliver the drinks in person. Harry took his and downed the contents in a

Dream, Baby

single shot. 'Now, that's "swallowing" man!' he grinned, as the barman made off with the empty glass. 'Well look, I'll tell you what happened,' and he removed his glasses once more, leaned one elbow on the table and adopted a studious demeanour.

'Nothing!' he giggled, then, making a determined effort to appear serious, he continued, 'Not till the next morning anyway. You have to use the drug before you sleep, obviously.'

'Obviously,' parroted Jamie.

'Then I went to bed and I dreamed and next morning I remembered everything and my life changed forever...er, man,' he added, as if the imperative to use that term needed occasional reinforcement.

'So I see. And, what was it you remembered?'

'What I would otherwise have forgotten,' responded Harry, enigmatically.

'Which was?' It showed signs of being a long evening.

'Which was: the understanding that my whole life was a sham! All those emotions from which my mind had protected me nightly; all those ghastly realisations about repressed ambitions and inhibited desires that it had secreted away in the mistaken belief that it should protect me from myself, prevent me from deviating from the path mother nature had considered wise for our species.

'And then it was all gone and I saw the real me and I can tell you, it was a bit of a shock!'

'I imagine it was.' Jamie stared thoughtfully at the space above the table. Corinth extricated herself from Harry right arm, murmured, 'See ya babe,' and slid off into the gloom. Harry examined the bean necklace between be-ringed fingers.

'I take it the Nobel Prize is a no no, then?' volunteered Jamie.

'Oh, yeah, sure thing.' Harry stretched back and closed his eyes. 'I could get you a slug of the orchid

Fifty Percent of Infinity

juice though,' he whispered, 'if you wanna uncover the inner man, man.'

Jamie grimaced in the dark. 'Kind of you, Harry, but I think I'll stick with the nine to five, just for the time being...man.'

You Have One New Message

Nigel fiddled with the unfamiliar lock, pushed the door open with his knee and gratefully deposited the two straining carrier bags of groceries onto the hall's tiled floor. The agent's particulars had enthused on the proximity of the local supermarket but had overlooked references to the effort required in transferring purchases, on foot, from one location to the other. That, he supposed ruefully, they took as read, understandably making little allowance for single, first-time home-owners, who had hitherto relied on others to perform all their housekeeping duties.

He rubbed at his fingers, red and creased from the pressure of the carrier's plastic handles and then re-hoisted one of the bags and made for the kitchen.

As he passed the window's alcove he saw the persistent pulse of the answer-phone's red indicator light and, leaving his purchases propped against a kitchen stool, he returned to the hall and lifted the phone from its cradle.

'You have one new message,' intoned the machine voice, 'to hear your message, press three.'

He complied and waited. There was no message but nor was there the hum of white noise associated with an open line or the familiar burr of the dialling tone. Rather, there was what Nigel could only think of as an absence of sound, a silence strangely indicative of empty space. It was like opening the door into a vast and unlit cave. Somehow, without any apparent sensory input, he felt aware of a colossal void, stretching to infinity in all directions. Foolishly apprehensive he thrust the receiver back into its dock and stepped back from the alcove, to add distance to his action.

After a moment or two he shook himself, grinned like a fool at his reflection in the mirror above the phone and stepped back along the hall to retrieve the second bag of shopping.

'Stupid idiot!' he scolded himself, as he lifted the cans and packets onto the kitchen table and began the process of allocating a purpose to each of the bare cupboards and unfilled drawers. 'On your own for half a day and you're already getting paranoid!' Bloody unsolicited calls - probably from Bombay or somewhere trying to sell him accident insurance. That would be it; he'd read that they had automatic dialling in those places and if the system reached your number it rang regardless of anyone being available to speak to you. Maybe that was the sound of an open satellite connection. Amazing really. Once upon a time you had to book-up a week in advance to get a trans-Atlantic hook-up and now some half-baked Karachi call centre could waste time ringing you via a device in orbit a thousand miles above the Earth.

He relaxed at the thought of some salesman from the sub-continent missing his bonus in that manner but was still unsettled by the sight of the message light blinking out its silent announcement the next time he returned to the hall.

Frowning, he raised the phone to his ear and pressed the button.

'You have one new message. To hear your message, press three.'

New message? There couldn't be a new message; he'd only been a few paces away since the last time the light had summoned him and he'd certainly have heard the ringing of an incoming call.

He pressed three.

You Have One New Message

And was like a man hanging, gravity-free, a thousand feet high in absolute darkness. His eyes told him he was there, in his new home, his feet firmly planted among the intricacies of the Victorian tile-work; the open kitchen door revealing a worktop still strewn with tins of bean and boxes of cereal; the traffic of an ordinary day visible through the stained-glass panels of the front door. But his mind, his subconscious, fought against vertigo and the terrible, all-consuming fear of a place without boundaries, and of a scale beyond his comprehension.

He pawed at the receiver, clenching it between his palms to depress the keypad and end the call and, as the terrible awareness faded, he threw the thing down and ran back to the stairs, where he sat breathing heavily and fighting for calm.

He sought to fill his mind with other considerations. What did he know about this place, his new home? Terraced, Victorian, two up, two down - if you didn't count the kitchen and bathroom and they were so small as to be barely worth counting. What else? Five minutes from the supermarket - oh yeah. Five minutes from the bus stop - yet to be tested. Low rent because the landlord was anxious to re-let, because...because... the previous tenant had done a bunk? No, vanished, without trace. Possibly done a bunk. Some sort of scientist. Quantum physicist, Google said. Working in 14 dimensions. Sounded like bunk from the man who'd done a bunk! Was that relevant? And to what? To the phone message that wasn't a message?

He became aware of a small point of reflection in the front door's brass knob. A tiny, distorted, convex view of the hall and stairway and deep within the image, a miniscule point of red light, flashing, flashing, flashing.

'You have one new message. To hear your message press three'

Fifty Percent of Infinity

He had no will to resist. The invisible night opened up around him once more, the primeval fear of dark places poured into his psyche. He stood, unmoving in the hallway, whilst his inner self thrashed wildly for handholds, for footholds - and found none. Once again, he dashed the phone from his hands and sought the reassurance of his reflection in the mirror. But the glass surface had become a portal onto a wide, cold starscape and beyond the hall's leaded widows a frosty darkness flowed past.

Affair of the Heart

Mr Brownshaw was anxious. He had been summoned to his doctor's Harley Street consulting rooms by an early morning call, which had been short on specifics but insistent with regard to the urgency of his situation. One phrase in particular might have quickened his pulse, had his heart still responded to the appropriate stimuli but now, the organ in question purred smoothly on, it's bio-mechanical processes untroubled by glandular secretions.

'Your secretary said it was a matter of life and death,' he said, his voice trembling just a little despite his heart's indifference to endocrinal activity.

Sir Harvey Cranley-Smyth furrowed his brows to reflect his own concern and clasped his hands before his face, almost in an attitude of prayer.

'That was perhaps,' he ventured, at last, 'a not altogether appropriate choice of phrase.'

'Then it's not that serious?' Mr Brownshaw asked, hopeful anticipation flooding his mind in lieu of glandular relief.

'That's not quite what I meant, I'm afraid.' Sir Harvey leaned forward a little and looked directly into his patient's questioning eyes. 'It's not really life or death...' he paused, 'life isn't one of the alternatives I'm afraid.'

Mr Brownshaw stared back at his physician, panic finally inducing a response as his skin dampened and acid gnawed at his stomach lining.

Fifty Percent of Infinity

'But, but, you said things were going so well!' he said accusingly, 'that the heart was working perfectly! It's two weeks since my last visit. I feel fine, really well!'

'Yes, it is,' the surgeon insisted, 'working perfectly; the heart. The finest piece of bioengineering the world has ever seen. Quite amazing, really. Extraordinary; yes.'

For a moment he lapsed into silence, apparently examining the grain of the desktop, and then he raised his head again and continued, 'but that's not quite the point, you see.

"You'll remember I told you that your new heart was designed and constructed in the Polgrad University in Azrastan?'

' "The People's Republic of", yes, of course I do; it was an incredible breakthrough for their medical research department, you said. Biggest thing that had happened in their nation for centuries.'

'Correct. In fact, it's no exaggeration to say that the development of the synthetic heart might be the saviour of their entire economy.'

'So?'

'Well, naturally, they're very possessive about the technology. Taken out world patents, intellectual property rights, that sort of thing. And the point is...' Sir Harvey bit his lower lip and regarded the small, inoffensive man sitting across the desk, 'the point is that there was a God-awful foul-up in the paper work when your heart was exported and it seems it required the permission of the President, no less, and he didn't look favourably on the mistake at all. Chap responsible got into terrible trouble and, well, the thing is, they want it back.'

'Want it back! Want what back?'

'The heart.'

'But they can't have it back! The operation was irreversible; you said so!'

Affair of the Heart

'Well, that's not entirely correct.'
'Isn't it?'
'Well, no. The thing can be taken out.'
'But...?'
'You won't survive the procedure...but look!' Sir Harvey rushed on, quelling Brownshaw's urgent objection, 'you only had a few weeks left as it was. No, scratch that...a few days! Without the operation you'd be dead by now so at least it's bought you a fortnight's extra life.'

'A fortnight's extra...! I don't belief what I'm hearing! You can't write me off just for the scrap value!'

'Oh, come now old chap, it's more than that you know. Azrastan's economic survival and all that. Your sacrifice could mean the difference between life and death for hundreds of people; thousands maybe!'

'That's rubbish! One lousy heart can't matter to them. Even in Azrastan it must be petty cash!'

'Ah, but it's the principal, you see. The President believes that if one Western nation gets away with infringing their patents there'll be a free-for-all. He believes they have to make a stand.'

'Well, he can bloody well make it somewhere else! I shall speak to my MP!'

'Oh, I hope you will, because I'm sure he can explain the whole thing better than I. Downing Street will have briefed him thoroughly, I'm sure.'

'Downing Street?'

'Oh yes, the Prime Minister has been involved right from the outset. The Azrastan President telephoned him as soon as he heard about the...er, infringement.

'And the PM must have been appalled. Wasn't he? Appalled?'

'Oh yes, appalled's the word all right. He was just about to sign an arms deal with the country and the whole thing's been put on hold until...mmm...until the affair of your heart has been sorted out. So, he's keen on the thing being brought to a...a "speedy conclusion", I think that was his phrase.'

'Affair of the heart? You make it sound like a bloody romance! But there must be another way! What about the fella who filled out the wrong form in the first place? Can't they sue him or something?'

'Unfortunately, he met his end in a freak traffic accident the day after the news broke.'

'Freak?'

'Only 0.4% of the Azrastan population owns a car.'

'So wasn't he unlucky! They sound like a right bunch of cutthroats! What about you? You imported the damned thing.'

'Yes, you're right to show concern but the compensation should more than clear my expenses.'

'Compensation! You're getting paid for this fiasco?'

'Well, it wasn't my fault was it? I'm as much a victim in this debacle as you, aren't I?'

'No! I really don't think so! And I'm leaving - this very minute and there's nothing you can do to stop me!' and with those words, Mr Brownshaw pushed back his chair and stood defiantly for a second before turning to the door.

Oh, but I'm afraid there is, said Sir Harvey Cranley-Smyth, but silently, to himself and he reached for the desk-top computer which was running the program to monitor his patient's heart-rhythm and pressed the delete button.

After several minutes he reached for the switch on his intercom and spoke.

'Angela, send the porter through to my office, Mr Brownshaw has had an unfortunate relapse, and then cancel the rest of my appointments for the afternoon, I shall be busy in the theatre.

Mistaken Identity

'Why the heck did the little green men have to arrive on my watch, Sam?' Admiral Susan Wingate, tossed the printout onto the console and swivelled her chair round until she faced Flag Lieutenant Sam Pescod, who had been waiting patiently for a response to the signal he had delivered moments earlier.

'Write you into history, ma'am,' he replied, diplomatically.

'With footnotes, if I cock up the most important moment since Neil Armstrong put the first boot on the Moon. Need I remind you that we are three light years from Sanctum and High Command requires an immediate response? That means finding a ranking officer who can make planet-fall within what they might consider a reasonable time frame. Have we got any ships out there?'

It was the paradox of mankind's exploration of the cosmos that whilst the introduction of quantum tunnelling had enabled almost instantaneous communication over stellar distances, no such short cuts were forthcoming in relation to the macro-world. The fastest vessels could still barely attain fifty percent of light speed, so that journey times remained painfully slow when related to the vastness of space and the brief span of a human life. Expansion had consequently, been on a generational scale and confined to those quarters of the sky that had been most accessible with the technology available at any given moment in time.

Despite these limitations the search had been thorough and yet, despite a century and a half of space travel and the investigation of thousands of planets, hope of discovering another sentient race in the local arm of the home galaxy had all but disappeared. Life, yes, there was life aplenty, everything from bacteria to ape analogues but nothing approaching serious intelligence...until now.

On Sanctum, a small, unprepossessing planet, five hundred light years from Earth, micro-biologist Annul Risvic had crossed a ridge and found herself in the presence of an alien artefact.

'We're in luck!' the adjutant prodded the luminous column of statistics suspended before him. 'There's a cruiser just outside the system, if we can find someone suitable on board they can be planet-side in seven standard days.'

'Identify the cruiser.'

'Er, it's Army ma'am, out of the base on Foster's World.'

'Army!' the senior officer's tone was derisory.

'Yes, ma'am, but if I might suggest ma'am? There's no glory for the Navy; as you observe, we are too distant to take part in the action so, if there is to be a "cock up", better it's in the hands of the Pongos, don't you think, ma'am?'

'And if they come out smelling of roses? It's not such a difficult assignment after all. Just establish a peaceful rapport with the extra-terrestrial...'

'If it is peaceful, ma'am.'

The artefact was approximately cuboid and massive; a dark, oily grey with protuberances for which the crew of the scientific expeditionary ship, Nuts in May, could discern no obvious function. They scanned it in three dimensions, analysed it with a number of sensors, to no real conclusion, and retired to their own craft to report its presence to their research centre and to await developments.

Mistaken Identity

'Most of the crew of the cruiser are in cryogenic suspension, ma'am. I'll run through the manifest and see if there's a candidate for hero of the hour.'

'Do that. I've been given full authorisation to second any member of whichever force I choose.

'They're mostly squaddies, ma'am - no, strike that...ah, we may have our man.' The Lieutenant brought the scrolling list of names to a halt and pointed at the highlighted, central entry. 'Major Terry Graham CC, ACE, SAS, - served on Ganymede in forty-eight, that was a nasty little affair ma'am - what do you think?'

'Issue the order, Sam. They can leave him chilled, put him aboard a shuttle and set him to wake on touchdown. The Nuts in May crew can brief him on arrival. Job done. I wish Major Graham every success. Now, I intend to watch the rest of this encounter on the newscasts.'

Flag Lieutenant Pescod nodded, watched his senior officer vacate the control room, turned back to the display and began to compose instructions for the cruiser's acting captain. As he entered the details he paused and re-examined the glowing entry, his brows furrowing. Oh shit! He should have realised; the names were listed alphabetically, by surname, not rank. Holy Moses, the boss would have his balls for breakfast when she found out. He pulled a face. If, she found out he thought, with a grim smile, as he entered the name: Private, Terry Graham Major.

***

The Nuts in May had been hailed by the alien vessel within one standard time unit of its first sighting; the contact had been brief, consisting of a numerical sequence, which the computer aboard the human's vessel had been unable to decipher. The crew, on

Fifty Percent of Infinity

imparting this news to their home world, had been instructed to keep radio silence and await assistance.

'Major Graham, welcome to Sanctum. Boy, are we glad to see you!'

Annul rose from her desk and extended a hand in greeting as the figure before her undogged his helmet and blinked in the bright lights of the laboratory module.

'As you can imagine, this has been quite an unnerving experience for us all.' She freed her hand from his grasp and used it to indicate the two other occupants of the room: a thin, Nordic male with a wisp of sandy beard and a short, dark-haired woman. 'Andrik and Sonia. I'm Annul, I discovered the alien ship when I was out on a field trip - but I suppose you'll know all this? I imagine you've been pretty fully briefed en route. How do you want to play it from here on in? Will you try to establish radio communication or just march straight over and knock on their door!' She smiled in what she hoped was an engaging manner and raised her eyebrows questioningly.

'Where's yer kitchen, miss?' The man before her was in the act of removing his suit and had one foot stuck in the ankle clamp. He stumbled, finally shook it loose and stood, examining his surroundings.

'Our kitchen?' Annul's eyebrows lowered themselves into a frown. 'We only have the usual processor, why do you ask?'

'Well, I s'pose that's why I'm 'ere, in't it...t' cook for you guys?'

'Cook!' The man identified as Andrik, choked back a laugh. 'Not unless you're intending to serve up our friend from Ursa Major...er, Major.'

'Sorry mate, you've lost me there. Who's from Ursa Major?'

Mistaken Identity

'No one,' said Annul, scowling at Andrik, 'it was a joke, and not a very good one. We assumed you'd come to make first contact with the alien, sir.'

'Terry, just call me Terry. Alien? You got an alien? Gawd 'elp us! Are we safe? 'Ave you told the bigwigs?'

'I rather thought that was why you were here, Major...er, Terry - in response to our alert. They said they'd send the nearest experienced officer.' She frowned again and reappraised the station's visitor. 'Have they told you anything about the situation, sir?'

'Nuffin. One minute I wus in deep-freeze, the next I wus touchin' down 'ere, wherever 'ere is; and I'm not - an officer. I'm Private Terry Major, Spacefleet Caterin' Corp. The 'ead-up said as you'd fill me in on what wus expected, miss.'

'You're not Major Terry Graham?'

'I wish, miss! Nah, and Graham's me middle name.'

'But they sent us your biog. What about all those post nominals?

'Post whats, miss?'

'The letters after your name! All that CC and ACE and what about the SAS for heaven's sake! Did you fight in the Ganymede Offensive in forty-eight?'

'Fight? I should fink not! Blimey, it was 'ot enuff in the cook'ouse, wivout stickin' yer 'ead above the bloody parapet, 'scus my Martian, miss. A, C, E stands fer, Award fer Culinary Excellence and the S, A, S is Sweets 'n' Savories, cos that's what I majored in, if you'll excuse the use of the word, under the circumstances, miss. The C, C,...'

'...is the Catering Corp, yes, I get the picture, Private. So, someone's screwed up big time. What do we do now, I wonder?'

'That's up to the Navy's Sector HQ, Annul,' Sonia turned from the communications consul where she had seated herself during the conversation, 'apparently, they issued the order for the cruiser inception, so I suggest we politely inform them of their mistake and ask for instructions.'

'Why do I think we aren't going to like their reply?' wondered Andrik.

***

'He's WHAT?' Admiral Wingate bellowed, grasping the arms of her chair and half-rising from behind the desk.

'A private, ma'am,' Lieutenant Pescod made a valiant effort to retain his composure and added, 'a cook, ma'am...first class.'

He might have got away with it, he thought, if the damn squaddie had been some battled-hardened warrior type, someone with experience of front-line duty; but a bleeding cook! And that string of letters after his name had sounded so impressive.

'First class?' The Admiral was on her feet now, fists planted on the desk, body leaning menacingly towards her aide de camp. 'FIRST CLASS! Oh, well that's all right then isn't it? He can whip up a bloody omelette for old E.T. and there'll be peace and harmony throughout the bloody cosmos! What in the name of all that's holy did you think you were doing Lieutenant? This is possibly the most important moment in the history of mankind - pending the Second Coming - and you've turned it into a flour-fingered, fuck-up!'

She sank back into her chair and pushed her own fingers through her hair. 'You really are an idiot Sam,' she said, in a more conciliatory tone, 'and I don't see that there's very much we can do but work with what we've got.'

'There's the crew of the Nuts in May, ma'am; they're scientific types, couldn't they take the reins?'

'They're civilians, Lieutenant. Can you imagine what High Command will say if I hand over the operation to them? - and besides, there's no certainty they'd agree to take responsibility. No, Private Major is the man we've sent in and he'll have to see the operation through to the end. If all goes well, we can claim foresight and intuition led us to select him.'

'And if it doesn't?'

'You can volunteer for the front-line in the intergalactic conflict. Now, issue the order, but Lieutenant, I want a visual link set up and maintained at all times and I want experts on hand to advise us every step of the way. I suppose it would be a good idea to include an anthropologist. Get someone patched through from Old Earth. They may be able to interpret the alien's body language or discern its cultural inclinations.'

'Meaning what, ma'am?'

'I have no idea, Sam. I have no idea.'

***

Private Terry Graham Major, CC, ACE, SAS, stood forlornly before the rising bulk of the first non-human structure which any of his race had ever seen and wished, fervently, that he was somewhere else.

The strangely interlocking plates glinted slickly in the pale light of the distant sun and thin skeins of silvery vapour roiled among the recesses and angular projections that covered the vehicle's surface. If it was indeed a vehicle, in any sense which the private, the crew of the nearby exploration vessel, or the small group of people watching back at Navy HQ via fermionic link, would have understood the term. After all, no one had seen it arrive at its present location and nothing about its construction gave any hint as to its method of propulsion, should one exist.

The private however, was giving no thought to these considerations as he clutched his shoulder bag of

Fifty Percent of Infinity

utensils and waited nervously for the edifice to grant him entry.

'I still can't see why he insisted on taking that load of kitchen equipment with him just to say hello to old bug-eyes,' murmured Andrik, as the three clustered around the viewer and watched the scene transmitted from the private's shoulder cam.

'He just feels more confident carrying the tools of his trade,' said Annul, sympathetically. 'Personally, I'd have let him take the kitchen sink if it made him any happier about going over there; besides, he has some sort of plan about finding common ground and he may have a point there - we all have to eat.'

'As long as we aren't eating each other,' observed Andrik. 'If it was me, I'd be very worried about being asked to dinner by the big, bad wolf. After all, we haven't a clue about the alien's intentions. We can't be sure that the Navy's computers have deciphered that string of code correctly. Is it really an invitation to go onboard?'

'Well, I don't believe there was any mention of dinner,' said Sonia, 'but I'll tell you one thing, there are some very large knives in that bag, so maybe our Terry can look after himself.'

'I hope so,' said Annul, worriedly, 'I do hope so.'

***

The classic scenario demanded some kind of doorway: a sliding panel, a circular iris, perhaps a ramp. In the event, the ship, if such it was, simply turned itself inside out.

No, not "simply", Sam Pescod corrected himself. The procedure was anything but that. In some unfathomable manner a portion of the construction altered its configuration and revealed an interior space,

Mistaken Identity

twenty metres high and wide and recessing twice that distance into the body of the machine.

Within it, behind a large, oval table, sat, or stood, or reclined, the alien.

It was oily grey, like the ship, and most resembled a mating of an octopus and a cockroach that had grown too big for its exoskeleton and had oozed between the intersections of its carapace. There were multiple limbs, some jointed, some more fluid in their construction, and the head - Sam swallowed, it must be a head he supposed - was a flurry of moving parts: mandibles - waving filaments - pulsing, translucent appendages. Above these, huge, multifaceted eyes rippled with rainbow colours. As he observed all these things, a voice hissed from the communication's console.

'Come, move, step, approach, here, toward, now, in calmness, freely.'

The words emanated from somewhere other than the being itself and were clearly the product of sophisticated software working on collected data.

Terry Major took a step forward and stared into the eviscerated construction. All around the alien the walls and floor bristled with mysterious equipment. By comparison the table that it faced was a wide, empty space, save for a bowl let into the surface near one end, containing what appeared to be a selection of leaves and a gherkin-like vegetable. In short, the private decided with some satisfaction, what the space most resembled was a kitchen.

'Listen, watch, observe, view, witness,' instructed the voice, drawing his attention back to the central figure.

'It's insectoid - well, you can see that,' Sam Pescod whispered in Terry's ear. 'The experts here say that the broad, flat mandibles suggest a vegetarian diet, so that's good news! Advice currently is not to make any sudden moves.'

The alien was "speaking" again.

'I, we, us; make, inform, decide. Group, collection, hive-father; maximum, teller, ruler, monarch, tell, collection, where, how; because of, greater force, pattern, modus, one mind, consciousness, embrace, encompass all, I, we, us. Strict, unbroken, way, determine, control, shape, rule I, we, us. Distrust, uncertainty, risk, enmity, conflict, war; I, we, us, you. Not trust, not risk, not live, you.'

The voice fell silent for a moment and the private stood, unsure what he should do in response.

'Best bet here,' Sam told him, 'is that it's telling you that it makes the decisions around here, on behalf of some kind of collective. Maybe it's this "hive-father" that was referred to. We don't like the sound of the last bit though; it may be saying something like, "this town ain't big enough for the both of us". There's clearly a lack of trust. We need a gesture to show empathy.'

'Empafy?'

'Fellow feeling, mutual understanding, that sort of thing.'

'Well that's easy enuff! Vegetarian did y' say? Lucky I brought along a nice bit a green salad frum the hydroponics and the ingredients fer a dressin' ain't it. They say the way to a feller's 'eart is frew 'is stomach, don't they? Watch and learn mate, watch and learn!'

With that, the private walked forward and climbed onto the exposed floor of the exploded room.

'Private, belay that move! Jesus, it's too late!'

As the soldier advanced a selection of the various devices adorning the walls and floor had reared up, illuminating or otherwise showing signs of an intention to repel borders.

'Steady! Look, I ain't got nuffin in me 'ands.' Terry laid his bag down carefully on the table top and held up both open palms to display that he was, as claimed, unarmed. "Ere, I'll just take one or two fings outta me

Mistaken Identity

bag, real slow, OK?' He removed two plastic boxes and a glass jar. The room's fittings withdrew a margin. Terry opened the boxes, located a small dish, poured oil and vinegar, located a shallot and rummaged in the bag, withdrawing a knife. The fittings hissed and extended their reach. 'It's just fer the onion!' Terry told them, displaying the vegetable between thumb and forefinger. Then he placed it on the table and angled the knife over it for a second before his hand became a blur and the onion collapsed into a score of thin slices. 'Not bad, eh?' he grinned, stacking the slices and repeating the action twice, first to produce strips then to dice those into tiny cubes of flesh. He did the same with a clove of garlic and stirred the ingredients together. 'What we could do wiv is somefink to add t' the salad,' he told his listeners, as he located the lettuce and placed it in a second, larger receptacle. He was away now, the locality and the circumstances of his preparations forgotten as he eased into the old familiar activity. 'This'll be perfect,' he announced, reaching for the gherkin-like object in the table-top bowl and in another blur of movement reducing it to a pile of paper-thin slices.

The shout had died on Sam's lips before it was uttered. With the final pivot of the blade a hundred tendrils had wrapped themselves around the private's legs and a dozen other shapes had arced up to aim at his heart.

'What's 'appened?' wailed the captive cook.

'We're very much afraid,' the voice in his earbud told him, 'that you have just sliced and diced the alien's supreme ruler.'

***

'Distinguished Service Star! Well done ma'am, congratulations.'

Fifty Percent of Infinity

'I hope Sam that you are not about to lay claim to a part of this award? It is, after all, a very thin line between the Empire's grateful thanks and court martial.'

'Wouldn't dream of it ma'am. Glory is all yours ma'am. Only too pleased to have lived to tell the tale, so to speak.'

'Well, if I were you, I wouldn't tell the tale at all, Lieutenant. I'd keep very quiet about your role in the whole affair. As it is, High Command seem content that we chose our representative wisely and that you played a pivotal part in the cementing of good relations between species, and no doubt you will earn an appropriate reward in due course. I may even recommend you as second-in-command on my new posting as Admiral responsible for Alien Liaison. How do you fancy a visit to Quesraquaddal?'

'I understand that is only the nearest equivalent of which the human tongue is capable ma'am, is that correct? But no, I think not. One close encounter is quite enough. I confess that the Quesra's life cycle is not one that I find attractive.'

'Xenophobia is in itself somewhat unattractive, Lieutenant and, as things turned out, it was fortunate that the Quesra undergo a larval stage in their development to adulthood or we might all have found ourselves on the front line.'

The Lieutenant nodded. 'Mmm, like everyone else I'd assumed it was the "roach" that was addressing us. When our expert suggested that he might just be the pilot and that the "gherkin" was really the big cheese - if you'll forgive me for mixing my culinary references, ma'am - it was too late to stop young Major from chopping his way through the "King of the Quesra". Lucky the Captain's response was only reflexive and soon withdrawn, although the Private got some nasty burns nevertheless.'

Mistaken Identity

'The Quesra were most apologetic. Especially as executing the Emperor-in-waiting was seen as a symbolic act, which freed them from another century of enslavement. Curious evolutionary path; who'd have guessed that the larval stage was the dominant and most aggressive and the final adult form so benign.'

'I still can't see why they didn't bump him off themselves, if his dynasty had been that unpopular.'

'Honour, Lieutenant. Honour and a thousand years of adherence to a code of behaviour which was their real enslavement after all. The Quesra evolved from a hive community; no independence of thought. It was only our intervention which forced change upon them. You misread a file entry and altered the course of Quesran history. It's a strange old life. By the way, what happened to Private Major?'

'Left the service ma'am. Made a fortune selling his story to the newscasts. Opened a restaurant on Diadem II, the so called, paradise planet.'

'Very nice too, although I had thought he might try his hand on Quesra; he's quite a hero there, as you can imagine.'

'Yes ma'am, but apparently he couldn't stand the food.'

Fifty Percent of Infinity

End of the Line

Path sat on the promontory and surveyed, in a detached manner, the scene below him.

There was activity wherever he looked: vehicles arriving and departing as they made the short journey from the wrecked shuttle to the base camp, figures loping to and fro in the low gravity, the world's yellow sun throwing violet shadows across the bare rock. In the space of just a few waking periods a small town had already risen from the empty desert. Tall, metal storage towers; squat, transparent living quarters; conglomerations of machinery and electric cabling whose purpose he could not fathom. By the time his world's moon had circled the skies a dozen times, the bipeds would possess this planet and the civilisation of the Raths would be forgotten. No, not even that, he realised, with an amused flick of his blue tongue across his scaly lips; not merely forgotten but unrecognised, unknowable, irrelevant.

The new colonisers would find no indication of an earlier occupation; no ruins, no detritus, no trace whatsoever of his dynasty. All that had existed had been swallowed by convulsions of the earth; buried beneath cooled, grey lava. He swept his armoured tail over the dusty outcrop and stared out across the fern-covered hillside. He was the last of his kind and the newcomers had inherited his kingdom but he knew that their rule would be short-lived. They were too few and within a dozen generations their skills would be forgotten and their descendants would be no more than animals foraging for survival, their technology rusted and lost, like that of his own people.

He turned his back on the valley and moved off towards the distant shore. The end of his line: the last of the dinosaurs.

Living in Realtime

It was some months since I'd visited the professor and I was dismayed when I saw the neglect that had overtaken his garden. His once lovingly tended rose beds were overgrown with weeds and the previously immaculate lawns were unkempt, with dandelions flowering amongst the ankle-deep grass. There were signs too of abandonment within the house. As I approached the door I saw that the curtains had been carelessly pulled across grime-encrusted windows and cobwebs festooned the leaded casements. I stood on the threshold, my hand on the knocker and hesitated, wondering what could have occurred to bring about this decline in my old friend's circumstances. Had he been ill? Surely someone from the faculty would have been in touch. Was it simply a matter of advancing age? My former tutor must, by now, be well into his eighties and his independent nature might have led him to shun assistance and struggle on alone. With these thoughts in mind it was with some foreboding that I finally sent a series of sharp percussions sounding through the house and stood, waiting as their echo died away and silence returned to the cottage.

Some minutes passed while I gave due consideration to the old man's imagined frailty and then I struck again, this time with more force and determination. Once again, the sounds faded away and a deep quiet fell all around. Was deafness an additional burden of his advancing years? I pressed tentatively at the door-handle and, finding it unresisting, turned it and pushed gently at the heavy oak panels. The door gave a little

Fifty Percent of Infinity

and I widened the gap and peered into the hallway beyond.

It was just as I remembered it: the uneven walls painted in a warm yellow, the age-blackened beams tilting deliciously from the vertical. The tapestry-seated bench, rack of walking-sticks, pan-handled barometer and, at the passageway's further extremities, the enticing flood of light from the left, where lay the sitting room and its wide, south-facing windows.

That latter encouraged me. The shrouded nature of the other windows had been depressing, suggestive of someone withdrawn from the world and shunning intrusion, but the thought of the old, sun-filled lounge with its view of the nearby Downs, recalled previous, happy visits when we had talked and debated long into the summer evening and shared a glass of claret as the sky deepened and the stars filled the Sussex sky.

Emboldened by this thought, I pushed the door fully open and stepped inside, shouting as I did so the professor's name, in a voice loud enough to summon him even if he should be at the most distant reaches of his domain. Reply came there none.

I moved further down the hallway, searching the stairway and landing as I passed and at last stood on the threshold of that inner sanctum which I recalled so fondly.

To my amazement, the professor was within, seated at his desk and watching me with a curious eye as I entered the room and greeted him with enthusiasm and some little relief.

'Professor! How good to see you. I hope you will forgive me for entering without invitation but I wasn't able to make you hear.

'Are you quite well?' I added, as my old friend continued to stare uncomprehendingly in my direction.

'Damn!' he exclaimed, finally, leaning back and regarding me over steepled hands, elbows resting on

Living in Realtime

the maroon leather arms of his captain's chair. 'I had not expected to see you again.'

I was taken aback at this response to my appearance. It seemed hardly welcoming.

'Why ever not?' I asked, the idea surfacing at once that he was indeed so unwell that he had not expected to survive until my next circuit.

He offered no reply to this, merely continued to hold my gaze with hooded eyes and a frown that was more suggestive of a puzzle unsolved than of distaste for my presence in his sitting room.

'I couldn't phone,' I explained, 'didn't know I'd be in your neck of the woods until I was already en route. Got a call from Cavandish, asking me to attend an unexpected seminar and realised it took me through the village.'

Still he sat, unmoving, regarding me thoughtfully. After what seemed like an age he lowered his hands, gave a resigned smile and focused, properly on my face.

'You,' he began, 'are a manifestation of my inner doubts. Doubts,' he continued quickly, to avoid any interruption, 'which I believed I had eradicated but which I now see are more deep-seated than I had thought. Fascinating!'

What game is this, I thought, for I was certain now that it was a game; some sort of intellectual challenge with which I was being invited to engage. The professor had adopted this modus operandi during his philosophy tutorials at the university, throwing us off balance with sudden mis-directions and non-sequiturs designed to make us think for ourselves, instead of merely following the great man's lead.

'I never knew you had inner doubts, Professor,' I said, obsequiously.

'Ha! As the source of that revelation it hardly behoves you to deny their existence, my boy. Very well, for the sake of confirming my faith in metaphysical solipsism I will use you as a sounding board. Your continued presence or otherwise will be a marker of my success.'

Solipsism? I trawled my memory of philosophical concepts and uncovered a definition. Solipsism was the idea that only your own mind existed and that the real world, and even other minds, had only a possible existence that must remain unproven. Metaphysical solipsists, if that was the correct noun, took things a whole step further and propounded that the world and everything in it were inventions of the self. There were several other degrees of supposition in this regard but the one to which the professor had just laid claim as an adherent, was the most extreme and, if accepted completely, meant that the believer was the single mind in existence, and everything in the "real" world was simply in their imagination!

'Are you about to tell me that I'm a product of your mental processes,' I asked.

'Most certainly! I know it to be so. Half a century of study has shown it to be so. Oh, it's a difficult enough state to comprehend but that's just the point. When the imagined world is so comprehensive in its construction, detaching one's self and seeing it from without, is mind-yearningly difficult. It requires a complete withdrawal from all sensory and mental input which references that false existence. Only then can one see the true nature of what one's mind has brought into being.'

'And that's your mind, is it?' I said, petulantly, 'Not mine, or the mind of the guy at the petrol station up the road. Just you, making personal decisions about the structure of the universe?'

He arranged his features into what I can only describe as an enigmatic configuration and said nothing.

I still believed I was being tested, or at least, used for the professor's amusement. I couldn't bring myself to

Living in Realtime

accept that he truly thought of himself as some kind of supreme being.

'Doesn't that make you God?' I asked, to explore that point, 'if all this,' I gestured around me and out towards the line of hills, 'is your creation?'

He was dismissive. 'Hardly! "All this," as you term it, is below God's pay grade - as your friend Cavandish might put it. I'm not laying claim to whatever it is that exists outside of my imagination, and certainly not to my own existence, I'm merely acknowledging that everything I see around me, including yourself, is the product of my own mental activity. '

'Merely! Now who's being flippant with his terminology? It sounds like a pretty big claim to me, dismissing me as a figment of your brain's inventive capabilities. So, tell me what I was doing this morning! Presumably my agenda is organised by you, if you really are in control of the world.'

He smiled grimly at that, obviously relishing the argument. 'Do you know about the eye,' he asked, mischievously. It was a familiar gambit: distract your opponent with a sudden change of direction.

'The eye?'

'Yes, did you know that a considerable percentage of what you think you see in your peripheral vision, isn't actually being recorded, in detail, by the retina? It's "assembled" by the brain, from information it already holds.

'I'm not sure I see the connection.'

'Well, you're a construct of my brain's processing power. A sub routine, if you like, running in the background. The data's there if required but not essential to the main program.'

'That's bunkum! I know what I had for breakfast, but you don't and you can't access the information unless I tell you.'

'Ah, but that's just how I do access the information: I get you to tell me! It's information retrieval, it doesn't mean that you really have an independent life, just that all the necessary code has been written enabling me to download the details! You'll tell me now that you remember eating bacon and eggs, kissing your wife goodbye, filling up with four-star at half past eleven in that Esso garage off the motorway slip road - but it's all part of the illusory world I've built for myself. Your belief in memory is part of that construction. You can't really have done those things because there is no real world in which they could take place!'

My God! I thought, he really believes these things! It's some kind of intellectual dementia! Paranoia built on a lifetime of abstract thought.

'Listen,' I said more gently, easing myself into the chair opposite his own, 'let's say all this is true - there's no reason it should change your life. What you've "imagined" has been OK up until now, hasn't it? The world you've constructed has been a good one, wouldn't you agree?' I was remembering that overgrown garden, the grubby windows. I could see now that the professor had withdrawn from what he perceived as a world of artifice and false hope. How could I have overlooked his emaciated frame, gaunt features, hollow eyes? For the first time I looked more closely at our surroundings and saw there the squalor and disrepair: the dirt-smudged carpets, the thick layer of dust on every surface, the flaking plaster. I had called just in time. Medical intervention might at least ease his remaining days.

A movement brought my attention back to the sad figure before me. He had pulled himself more erect, dropped his hands below the desk; all at once his features seemed to display a new urgency.

'A good world?' He spat out the words with a mixture of disgust and despair. 'A lifetime of study and

Living in Realtime

introspection, and where has it led me? To the realisation that it's all been flim flam and fakery! And you think I should be satisfied with that? I've searched for understanding of the human condition and found that it's whatever I choose it to be! There are no profound truths, no meaning to life because there is no life! I think, therefore I am! But where I am is as unknown as when I started out sixty years ago! Your arrival is by design, a sort of visual metaphor for a tiny, remaining uncertainty about the next step I plan to take. But your inability to present a meaningful contradiction simply confirms the action. It's time to wipe the slate, begin a new journey, discover where "self" truly resides.'

Suddenly he lifted his hands from his lap and I saw that one of them held a gun. As I leapt towards the desk he lifted it briskly to his mouth and jerked his index finger once. The faded floral print of the curtain was suddenly suffused with a new splash of crimson, although from where I stood, the professor looked more at peace than at any time since my arrival.

I gagged, controlled the reflex, stepped back and turned away to survey the peaceful, untroubled countryside. A mist had fallen on the Downs, obscuring their outline, the wooded middle-distance already fading with the encroaching evening. I lifted the phone but there was no tone, tried for my mobile but found no signal. When I looked up again the fields and nearer trees were already lost to sight. I looked back to the professor's body and imagined the dying brain: the synaptic pathways constricting, the electronic patterns losing coherence, one by one.

In moments, brain death would finally claim the man who believed himself to be my creator and any program his mind had written for me would decay and vanish in a cloud of particles. I was saddened by the thought that more than a half century of work had culminated in such delusion, although, I reflected, maybe each of our minds had its centre and the professor's story was written in code on my own cortex. Just perhaps, he was my creation, rather than I, his.

Slow Lane

Let me start by asking you a question. If your best friend told you, after the third round of drinks at the bar one evening, that he had discovered the secret of immortality, would you believe him?

And, before you answer, confident as I am of your denial, let me correct a deceit, which has already crept into my unlikely narrative. Chris - I shall call him Chris, although that was not his name - Chris did not, in fact, claim to have uncovered the secrets of eternal life, personally. No, he attributed this amazing breakthrough to his uncle, a man of whom I had often heard him speak, but who I had never met and whose very existence I had long since come to doubt.

Uncle Quentin, again a sobriquet, was, I was almost sure, a figure of fiction; a character conjured up by my friend in much the same way that a young child invents a mythical playmate. Uncle Q was the focus of both admiration and frustration; he was the butt of jokes, the target of criticism, an example to which we all should aspire and a representation of everything we might best avoid. He was, in short, a useful way for Chris to express opinion and preference without admitting ownership of either.

Or at least, that was what I had come to believe until that evening in Clancy's Bar.

My friend was by no means drunk but several pints of the local hop had freed him of his natural reserve and brought him to a state where he seemed anxious to share a confidence.

Fifty Percent of Infinity

And that's when he told me about his uncle's research into longevity.

The old boy had a facility somewhere up in the mountains. The money came from a huge bequest left to him by a former collaborator and he had insisted that it was as remote and inaccessible as possible to ensure absolute secrecy. He was working, he said, to develop a serum that would slow the ageing process but by a cruel irony he had found his own life cut short by cancer. When the confirmation of his condition came through, he closed up the laboratory and checked himself into hospital, but first, he wrote to his nearest living relative, giving full instructions on how to reach the research centre and where he had secured the results of his studies, and hinting too at a darker side to his research.

That relative was Chris and the reason for his bar room disclosure was to tell me that he intended to travel to Uncle Q's lab and he wanted me to go with him.

I had an excuse, and to be honest, I was glad to be able to decline without recourse to lies and fabrication. I'd been offered my first job, two days drive from my then current home, and was expected to start work within the week. In fact, my purpose in meeting Chris that evening had been to say goodbye and wish him well for his own future. The story he was telling sounded like the ramblings of an old man whose impending death had turned his mind and I had no wish to hike into the wilderness to view the place in which he had been playing hermit for so long. So, I refused his offer and urged caution on his own behalf. Be careful what you're doing up there, I told him. Your uncle was probably nuts! He'd spent years on his own and heaven knows what delusions he was suffering. And remember his warning of a more sinister element to his work.

Slow Lane

That was the last time I saw Chris for over thirty years. My new work took up the whole of my interest to begin with and later, I moved on again, married and raised a family. I had forgotten entirely the story I had been told in Clancy's, until the day I was clearing the garage and found the old briefcase that I had purchased for my first placement, all those years before. Stuffed into one of the compartments was a beer mat on which Chris had scrawled a set of map references, 'just in case,' he had said, hopefully, 'you change your mind and decide to follow along.'

Out of interest I pulled out a map and checked the location. It wasn't so far from where Janet and I planned to spend our summer vacation, in a cottage loaned by a friend and so, inevitably, some weeks later, I found myself trekking through the foothills of a range of mountains which, for reasons you will soon understand, I am not about to identify.

Janet had begged off the hike with a migraine and so I was alone when I reached the vicinity of Uncle Q's facility. For a long while I was unable to find any sign of habitation and I had almost decided that even the laboratory had been a figment of a fevered imagination when I spotted an unusual symmetry about the foliage crowding a nearby defile in the rocks. On examination I discovered an ivy clad fence almost entirely consumed by undergrowth and, following its course for several hundred yards I came to a rusted metal door, entwined with vines and brambles. The lock had disintegrated years before but the ground beyond the entrance seemed blocked by an impenetrable barrier of thorn bushes and scrub.

I pushed against the corroded hinges and squeezed through into the dense mass of vegetation, turning my back and using my pack to shove aside the wiry branches and snagging briars. At last I broke free into a clearing of sorts and found myself standing before a formidable structure, like a concrete bunker with deeply recessed, steel-framed windows to left and right. Between them was another door but this one was a substantial construction with long, brass levers that yielded easily to the pressure of my hands.

In contrast to the wild confusion that lay outside, the interior of the building was neat and ordered. I walked along a dusty, tiled hall and, on my left, found a small but well-appointed laboratory. The equipment was tidily stowed, a white lab coat hung in its appointed place behind the door, but once again, every surface was shrouded in dust, the roof lights opaqued by dirt.

I returned to the corridor and examined the rooms to the right. One was a living space, comfortably furnished and decorated with once-colourful prints of seascapes. The next was a small office with a dark, wooden desk and an angled lamp.

The lamp was wreathed in cobwebs, as were the surrounding fittings and the figure bent over the desk, a pen clutched in its right hand, was Chris.

So overcome was I by the surreal nature of the scene that at first it was merely the presence of my one-time friend that arrested my attention. It was as if no more than hours had elapsed since his invitation to me and I had simply changed my mind about employment, marriage and family and had followed him here instead.

Then, as I stepped nearer, I realised just why the three decades seemed so fleeting. Chris looked exactly as he had in Clancy's Bar, a lifetime earlier: same unruly shock of auburn hair, same unlined features, clear eyes.

'My god, Chris...' I began, but the question died on my lips, because the figure before me was as stiff and unflinching as a waxwork; the eyes open and fixed on the page where the pen remained poised above the half-written script.

Slow Lane

I circled the desk and touched my fingers to his throat. To my amazement the skin was warm and yielding but I could discern no pulse. I snatched up a shiny, metal ashtray and held it close to his lips. Was there the slightest film of condensation? I couldn't tell.

As I stood, unsure what to do, I caught sight of the paper beneath the pen and the writing upon it. The heading, underlined for emphasis, carried my name.

I removed the page carefully and began to read:
"John,
FIRST - do not call for medical assistance!
Alert no one.
Read what follows before you do anything more.

I estimate that I need thirty years or so to complete this document so, if you have arrived earlier, you will never know the truth.

Listen, my uncle really had discovered the elixir of youth! And I have administered it with a mere prick of my thumb. But only then did I turn to his notes and discover the dreadful truth. I won't live forever - I'll live the usual three score and ten, or twenty, or whatever is the latest estimate of expectancy. The horror is that it will take me a thousand years to do it - maybe a hundred thousand - I've not made the calculation.

The serum slows the natural entropy of the cells, which means that every process which the body is heir to, takes place at a fraction of its natural pace. What my uncle realised was that this applies equally to the user's perception of the world. To me, in what seems a moment, hours pass by in the world around me. For two days after I administered the drug nothing happened and then, on the third morning I stood by the window and watched as in seconds, the trees shed their leaves, snow covered the hills and thawed in the spring warmth and the forest became green again with new growth. Clouds crossed the sky faster than I could follow their progress; and all the while night and day flickered across the landscape more rapidly than I could register.

It may take me most of your lifetime to write this so, if you come at all, it can't be too late. Help me John. Get someone to read my uncle's notes and see if the effects of the serum can be reversed. Please! And in the mean-time leave me here, where I'm safe from intrusion and misunderstanding. There's a deep well with endless supplies of water and my uncle had laid up a store of dehydrated foods and canned meals. But I can't tell how long they might remain edible and once open they putrefy almost before I can lift them to my mouth, as my seconds expend their days. Maybe y"

The writing ended with that single letter. I took the pen and wrote:

"Chris, I have found you. I will do all I can." And then I carefully replaced the paper beneath the raised pen. Presumably, from his point of view, my message appeared miraculously as he prepared to complete that last word.

That's all I could do. I closed the rusted door and hid it as best I could with branches, although I did not think it likely that others would discover it in so remote a spot.

That was a quarter of a century ago and I am an old man who has found no cure for my friend's predicament, although I have entrusted his future well-being to a government agency that has an interest in the development of the serum. One day soon I hope, he may find himself travelling at the same speed as his fellow men and, as I prepare for the end of my life, he can set out on the beginning of his.

End of Term

BelroogAdamSmyde expressed a silent wish for the pod's protective force field to de-opaque, and his neural implants, intercepting his brain's synaptic relays, responded and issued the command.

The view revealed, encompassed most of what had been known in later millennia as The Fraternity of The Middle Sea but which, in earlier chapters of the planet's history, had enjoyed a number of other appellations including, The Central Earth Confederacy and The European Union.

There was nothing now to suggest any such intervention and cooperation in mankind's affairs, indeed, from fifty thousand feet there was no indication that life had ever existed across the continent's scorched and desolate surface.

The suggestion of closer scrutiny ran through Adam's mind and, in answer, the craft, holding his body in a protective but invisible embrace, fell through the clear skies and took up a new station, one hundred feet above the ground.

Only a small segment of the sun showed above the Eastern horizon from this altitude but it still occupied a hundred miles of sky, its bloated form bathing the land in a wash of orange light.

This wasn't truly, "the end of the world", or even close. After a billion years, rising temperatures and evaporation had lowered carbon dioxide levels to a point where photosynthesis had become impossible and that had spelled the end, in one way or another, for most of the higher life forms. Now microbes had inherited the Earth, although even their time would come. Already the oceans were drying out and Adam could see the old coastline as a ridge of barren cliffs dropping to an arid wasteland of rock and desert where the central sea had once glistened under a friendly, yellow sun.

Adam had no memory of such a state of things; the human race had left the Earth millions of years earlier, migrating first to the outer planets and then after the intervention of the alien race, the Varaang, to the planets of other stars' systems. The Earth had been left to die slowly and the process, although well underway, was certainly not complete.

Mankind had thrived among the stars, expanding across the galaxy's spiral arm and, in the main, had forgot its origins on the blue white Earth.

In the main, but not the entirety. A society had arisen on one system, which, on the basis of a trove of ancient documents and the secret histories that they contained, had declared an allegiance to the birthplace of humanity, and vowed to keep its memory sacred.

No one knew when or by whom the texts had been created; their very survival after so immense a period of time was taken as a sign of their semi-mystical origins. The language they employed had taken decades to decipher and still the meaning of the words revealed eluded their greatest scholars, who remained convinced that, within the crumbling fabric of the box which held them, lay the key to understanding and controlling the very fabric of the cosmos itself.

It was a belief, Adam accepted, which required an act of faith, the true nature of the material lying forever beyond their understanding.

So, this was his personal pilgrimage: a visit to the old Earth. He induced a vision of the sacred box and it appeared, exquisitely detailed, rendered by the pod's projectors.

End of Term

He circled it - or let it circle him - the concept was uncertain when neither had a corporal reality, and he studied for the thousandth time the joints, the grain, the line of twenty symbols, divided by two equal spaces into three sets of decreasing number.

Only about the final set, was there some level of consensus; that together the five symbols conveyed a concept of unity, collective purpose, useful assembly.

The second set were the subject of controversy. Maybe they represented an activity, a pursuit or, as some few contended, a creative act - but what, they could not fathom.

And the first word? No credible interpretation had ever been volunteered. Adam studied again the eight indecipherable shapes with their linked verticals, diagonals and sinuous curves. Might they hold the clue to the meaning of life itself?

Adam, the last man on Earth, turned back to the pod's transparent wall and gazed out at the expanded sun, now filling a quarter of the sky, and at the dying Earth, its rocks splitting and flaking in the heat. Could the secret of the box hand him control of the very stuff of creation and the power to save the planet?

What was the "Group"? Who had been the "Writers"? And what in the name of all the gods was, "Midhurst"?

This story is dedicated to the members of the Midhurst Writers Group (based in West Sussex, England) who provided much of the inspiration and encouragement on which this collection of tales is founded. Will their collective output really survive until the world's end? Wait and see.

Fifty Percent of Infinity

Here Today

"...with this amazing app you can control your emotional state..." Larry closed his teeth over a forkful of pasta and, catching sight of movement beyond the uncurtained window, wondered, distractedly just where his twelve-year-old son was setting out for, this late in the evening.

"...just attach the stylish wrist sensor and key your preferred mood from your phone's onscreen menu..."

Larry turned his attention back to the new television for a moment, as his wife pushed through the door carrying a second plate of ravioli.

'Can you really do that?' he asked, as she seated herself across the table and busied herself with the Parmesan.

'Do what dear?'

'Alter your mood with a phone app? And look, where's Ben off to, on his bike? It's nearly half eight.'

'He's going over to Jack's to compare notes on their homework. Old Cartwright has set them a history project and I think they're both a bit unsure about how to begin.'

"...synch two bracelets and share your state of mind with your partner for a perfect..."

Larry frowned, 'surely, if you could do that...' he reached for his wineglass and drained what remained of its contents. 'Has he got lights on that bike?'

'Yes, of course he has'

'Right. Did you hear that, on the telly?'

'What dear?'

Fifty Percent of Infinity

'An advertisement for a phone app that's supposed to alter the way you feel. They can't do that, surely? We'd have heard something about it, on the news...wouldn't we?'

'Oh, they can do all sorts of things with their phones these days. Nothing would surprise me.'

'Yeah, but...' Larry took another mouthful of pasta and bit into it thoughtfully.

***

Next day, at work, Larry had asked Brian from IT about the curious commercial from the previous evening but Brian had just grinned and asked him what he'd been drinking and, when Larry had said, ho ho, red wine as it happened, Brian had asked him how many bottles and added that it was a great concept and he'd start working on it right away, ha ha, and maybe he'd be the next Mark Zucherberg! And Larry had laughed too and pretended it was a joke and had changed the subject.

***

That evening he had the house to himself: Karen at Pilates, Ben playing five-a-side at the local sports centre. Extracting the foil-wrapped meal from the oven, he opened a beer, placed the various accoutrements on a tray and made himself comfortable on the sofa before stabbing at the TV's remote, selecting the channel that had been running as he consumed his previous night's dinner.

During the first commercial break he watched carefully to see if the unusual phone device was featured but there were only the usual dreary announcements for butter substitutes and short-term loans. Larry finished his meal, carried the tray back to

Here Today

the kitchen, opened another beer and returned to the sofa.

In his short absence the regular programme had come to an end and, as he watched, *the credits faded and were replaced by the image of a car.*

"The Ford Secure, the driverless car with the extra touch of luxury..." Larry sat up straight, eyes fixed on the screen.

"...fitted throughout with planet friendly, lab-grown leather and featuring a holographic entertainment consul, this is the family transport module that runs for three-thousand miles on a single charge and..."

Larry gaped at the screen, jabbed at the remote, to verify the channel. What the hell was this? The set had retuned somehow, the numbers reallocated. He'd got a sci-fi channel instead of ITV...except that, there in the top corner was the identification marker.

"...take a test ride in the Ford Secure tomorrow and there's a chance to win the fully-immersive, VR VidCube, Journey to NASA's Luna Base. It's the simulated experience of a lifetime!..."

Larry squeezed urgently on another button; the ad for the impossible car flowed on, uninterrupted. He thumbed up and down on the keypad without effect, threw the remote down in disgust, crossed to the television and pushed the manual control. When that too failed to alter the programme, he jabbed the on off button. To his consternation, even this proved fruitless and he leaned down and wrenched the power line from the wall socket.

"...call tomorrow to set up an appointment with the new Ford Secure!..."

'Bloody hell!' What was going on? He strode to the window and looked out. The world appeared normal; the lights on in Number Three with Mrs M's daughter walking around her bedroom topless, again. He'd spoken to Mrs M about that, told her he'd got a teenage son for God's sake. Merv, washing his windows in the semi-dark: nutty as a fruitcake. Up the road two boys still kicking a ball about by the garages. Beyond them, the tree-shrouded hills surrounding the village were a dark silhouette against the last light of the dying day. He found a third beer in the fridge and downed it quickly, surveying the equally untroubled scene from the kitchen windows.

A change in the sound from the television made him return. A documentary was describing the setting up of the first Mars colony in 2068.

Maybe the beer was making him light-headed. He sank back onto the cushions and watched the screen as events unfolded. It wasn't right. You couldn't have TV without electricity. So, this had to be an illusion, didn't it? He considered, with a surprising lack of panic, the possibility that there was a tumour pressing on his brain, creating some sort of waking dreams. The narration droned on, soothing him into a comfortable sleep.

***

When he awoke he was struck at once, by the absence of sound. The television was silent, the screen unlit. From behind him, the half-light from the street suggested early morning. Had Karen and Ben left him to sleep, here, on the sofa? He struggled into a sitting position and took in the empty beer cans on the hearth. Maybe they had, at that. He yawned, stretched and stood, performing some improvised callisthenics before shuffling to the window.

The village scene remained untroubled, the only movement that of Cassidy at number forty-seven, loading his car with suitcases, presumably for another of his extended business trips. Surely his wife could see what he was up to? Everyone else in the estate seemed

Here Today

to know about his illicit affairs, how could she be so dumb? He stared into the street as his neighbour completed his preparations, climbed into the driver's seat and pulled away, up the hill, towards the main road.

Larry stood in thought for a moment wondering at the man's indiscretion and then, suddenly, the memory of the previous night rose into his mind and a frisson of excitement mingled with trepidation ran through his body. He walked across to the television and stared down at the unplugged power lead. The damn thing really had been running without electricity. Was that possible? Well, maybe it was, at that. He didn't really know much about the device. He'd bought it down at The Queen's one evening from a drunk who claimed to be an inventor, and had taken plenty of stick from Karen as a result. 'It was an unbelievable bargain,' he had told her in his defence, the next morning, when he'd sobered up.

'If it seemed unbelievable, it probably was,' she had retorted, continuing in the same vein for some considerable time. It was almost certainly stolen she had decided, or damaged beyond repair. Whichever, the man had seen him coming, or more accurately, had waited for Larry to get sufficiently inebriated to lose any sense of judgement.

He had accepted her admonition in a silence which had betokened an admission of guilt but when the set had been switched on, the picture had been clear and steady, the remote had run it through all the expected channels and even his wife had been forced to admit that there was little wrong with the equipment. She still held judgement as to its legal ownership, half expecting a visit from the local constabulary, but she had conceded that, just maybe, more by luck than judgement, Larry had secured an unlikely bargain.

Fifty Percent of Infinity

He smiled, smugly, and pulled the set away from the wall to examine the back. Batteries, that's what it must be; the thing had a battery back-up. But several minute's scrutiny failed to reveal a compartment lid or any indication of removable casing.

He pushed the television back into position and squatted before it, jabbing at the on/off button. A red light glowed into life on the forward edge and after a moment or two the screen illuminated and a picture formed. He glanced at the clock, saw that it was still only six and thumbed the sound down to minimum.

It looked like a news bulletin. He leaned nearer the set. The whispered voice of the announcer was describing a weather event as the pictures provided illustration.

"The drought continues in mainland Europe, with most of France now declared an emergency zone..." an arid landscape came into view, avenues of brown, leafless vines, the carcass of a long-dead animal. *"...parts of the country have been without water for over a year and the United Nations have instigated evacuation procedures for the whole of the central area..."* the picture switched to a long line of people, filing aboard a boat.

Larry heard a movement on the floor above and switched off the set. The voice droned on, the picture changing to show a different group of suffering humanity. Damn! Just how did you turn this thing off? He'd fallen asleep with it still running last night but this morning it had been silent. A timer? Funny idea for a TV. Funny? The whole thing was totally bizarre! He seemed to be watching scenes from the future...or a future anyway. And yet, he mused, the new car he had seen demonstrated last night seemed to be a part of a more affluent, less troubled world than the one currently depicted. If the set really was picking up signals from a time yet to come, did the period involved

Here Today

vary; one day the set finding transmissions from twenty-five years ahead, the next from a later century? And, was there any way he could benefit from owning this amazing piece of kit?

If he could just pick up, say, this weekend's racing results...?

Heck, bookmakers would accept bets on just about anything these days; who'd win elections, talent shows, the first snowfall. It didn't have to be a particular event, as long as he knew about it before anyone else! But he didn't want to have to wait till he was drawing his pension to get the pay-out. There must be some way of tuning the thing, surely. Karen had been watching the local news station a couple of nights ago so you must be able to select the day's date. He remembered now, she'd had some difficulty finding the channel. Had even suggested that was why he'd got the thing cheap! But she had found it in the end.

He listened for a moment; the noises upstairs had ceased. It was Sunday, he reflected, Karen wouldn't be up for an hour at least and Ben, well, there was no knowing when he'd appear, could be anytime up to midday. He crouched down beside the TV again and examined the controls. There was an old-fashioned rotating drum-switch on the right; he spun it experimentally. The picture flickered wildly. He moved it more slowly and the display altered with each turn. Something he recognised arrived on screen; he paused the action. It was a game show from a few years back; he watched in fascination for a few moments. His first spin of the dial had brought him back from the future, had overshot the present and had left him a decade behind his own time. He reversed the dial, moving it with care, watching each new programme for signs of familiarity. At last he was among more recent presentations. Some final, tiny adjustments found a picture of a current local BBC newsreader, the display on the wall behind showed 1800 hours and the day's date. It was that evening's news! Local sport would follow on shortly and, with the results information, he'd be in business!

Fifteen minutes later he put the phone down and grinned with satisfaction. All the money he had was riding on the outcome of a match for which he already knew the score line! He would be rich! They would be rich - although explaining his winnings to Karen might prove difficult. He could hardly tell her he had a magic television, and anyway, he had a sudden desire to keep the set's amazing capabilities to himself. If he just said he'd won the cash, she'd make his life hell, for taking the risk. Who cared? That was a bridge he'd cross when he came to it. In the meanwhile, the world was his oyster! It had occurred to him that he could dial the programme back at any time, milk it dry until current time and future time caught each other up. He could watch the whole bulletin from the beginning this time and see what other advance information he might exploit.

With utmost care he moved the dial, rediscovered the programme, sought the opening titles. It was disappointing. An interview with an MP, a piece about an engineering company closing down - that might have been useful with an earlier warning; insider information would allow him to trade on the market with no risk of being discovered - a campaign to save a crumbling pier. The next item concerned a tragic accident but it was only when the name of his own village was mentioned that he paid it full attention. A youth, knocked from his bike whilst making his way to a friend to share notes on his homework. Karen's answer to his earlier question about Ben leapt into his mind and his blood ran cold. The camera was focussing on a bloody patch of road whilst the voice-over told how the boy died at the scene from massive injuries.

Here Today

Larry stifled a rising panic. This was tonight's news, these things had yet to happen. Could the future be changed? It must be so!

He grabbed his keys, ran from the house, found Ben's bicycle, carelessly leaning against the garden shed. The car was on the drive, he waved the ignition to de-activate the locks, threw open the boot, jammed the bike inside and thumbed the lock button.

When he returned to the kitchen Ben was down, spooning cornflakes into his mouth.

'You're early,' Larry said, tersely, trying to dampen the hysteria he felt building within him.

'Yeah, gotta get down to the sports centre for early morning practice. It sucks.'

'I'll drive you down,' Larry announced on impulse, 'save you a bit of time.'

'That's a lame idea Dad, I'll have to walk back.'

'I can collect you too, I've er, gotta run inta town later for petrol. S'no trouble. What time you get finished?'

"Bout eleven-thirty.'

'OK.'

'Right, thanks.'

'No trouble.'

'You said that.'

He was no good at subterfuge. Karen looked at him quizzically when, later, he explained his offer to ferry Ben to and from the Centre.

'You usually have a drink with Ray on Saturday morning,' she said suspiciously, as she poured coffee, for a requested, early elevenses.

'Cutting back on the booze,' he replied, helplessly.

'Ha! Now I know something's up!' she snorted.

Ben spent the afternoon in his room, his father moving restlessly around the house and increasing his wife's suspicions. At four he emerged clutching a file. 'Gotta bike over to Jack's to finish off this stuff for

Fifty Percent of Infinity

Crapper Cartwright,' he shouted, taking the stairs three at a time,

'I'll drive you over,' called Larry, without considering the implications.

'Dad! For Chrissake's! I don't need you to hold my hand, thanks very much.'

'What is the matter with you?' Karen asked, appearing at the kitchen door. 'You've been twitchy all day. Are you looking for an excuse to get down the pub? You didn't stay on the wagon for long!'

'Hey, Mum, where's my bike?' A voice wailed from beyond the half-open front door.

'Bike? Wherever you left it,' Karen glanced up as Ben hurried back into the room.'

'Well, it's not there! Some goon must have stolen it last night!'

'Stolen? I shouldn't think so.'

'Then where is it!?' Ben was losing his composure now.

'I lent it to someone.' Larry, set his mouth firmly, in contradiction of his inner turmoil.

'Lent it? LENT it! S'my bike! You can't frigging lend it to anyone!'

'Lent it? Who'd you lend it to?' Karen was frowning now.

'Er, Ray, er, he had to be somewhere, that's why he wasn't in The Queen's this morning.'

'And he's forgotten how to drive has he? All of a sudden?'

'His car's in for a service,' said Larry miserably, sure that this latest invention would be found as wanting as his previous utterances.

'I don't frigging believe it!' Ben hurled his file across the room, scattering papers, and stormed up the stairs. Seconds later his bedroom door slammed shut with a force that dislodged a cup from the drainer.

Here Today

Larry grimaced and waited for Karen's next onslaught but inside he felt a relief at Ben's response.

Next morning whilst it was still dark, Larry removed the bike from the car's boot and leaned it against the house. Things would soon quieten down he told himself and once Karen had vented her anger at him for his stupidity in taking such an apparent risk with their savings, she would be unable to resist the lure of their new wealth. After that he had plans. He would tell her he was undertaking a series of investments and, when these proved successful, as they must, he knew she would come round. He climbed the stairs quietly, slid into bed and was soon back to sleep.

Everyone was up when he resurfaced, showered and shaved and headed downstairs. He had averted a terrible event and shown that the future could be changed. Now, he had only to collect his winnings and all would be wine and roses. He hummed a tune as he dialled the bookies number.

'Mr Holden, ah, yes, you're the gentleman who placed a considerable sum of money on United to lose three, two last night. My commiserations sir, you must be a very disappointed man this morning.'

'Disappointed?' A muscle in Larry's arm began to tremble, involuntarily.

'Well, six nil was pretty decisive, wasn't it sir? Hello, Mr Holden? Er, you were aware of the result sir...weren't you?'

Larry replaced the receiver, carefully. He had altered the future and his life had run onto a different track. He walked into the kitchen and stared across at his wife, dropping bread into the toaster.

'The bike's back,' she told him, with venom. 'So, I take it that whatever little game you and your mates got up to yesterday, it's all over now. I just hope the police won't be calling at our door.'

'The police...?'

Fifty Percent of Infinity

'And you might like to apologise to your son. You had no right to do what you did without asking him. You messed up his Sunday and probably ruined his chances of a decent mark in his history exam. At least he's been able to cycle over to Jack's this morning so they can try to finish the project before school.'

'Cycle...?'

"Yes, over to Jack's. What the hell is the matter with you, you look like you've seen your own ghost.'

A tear tracked down Larry's face. 'No,' he said, despairingly, 'I've seen my own future.'

Pick and Mix

'We meet every night, Peter, here in the laboratory.'

I was aware of him studying my face, gauging my reaction to this unexpected, and frankly disturbing, revelation.

It was six months since the accident, the night when all our lives had been derailed and his perfect contentment had been destroyed with the tumbling, crumpled bodywork and the insistent, billowing flames.

They had been a pair since childhood. Friends, then lovers and at last something more than that. A gestalt: two functioning as one and achieving, with that union, an insight that had brought them international fame.

They were - had been - physicists working at the frontiers of understanding. To me, a mere administrator, theirs had been obscure, unfathomable investigations into the multi-dimensional, quantum world. It made it all the more disconcerting to hear his answer when I asked, cautiously, how he was managing without her.

We all half expected to see his wife, each time we entered the research centre. Bryony with her red hair tied back in that familiar style, her technician's coat unbuttoned, her "serious" glasses sliding down her button nose. And sometimes, I found myself startled by a reflection that mirrored her movements, a remembered voice echoing down a corridor. But Bryony was dead: burned to ash when her car plunged from the flyover on a black night slick with ice.

Fifty Percent of Infinity

'You meet her?' I repeated, tentatively, 'you mean, in your mind?'

'No, Peter, I mean literally, each evening at eight o' four pm, in our laboratory.'

I'll admit, that my first thoughts then were as a facility administrator, research grants being somewhat reliant on the sanity of the recipient.

'You believe in ghosts?' I said, wholly incredulous.

He scowled. 'No! No, of course not...although,' he pursed his lips and sat in thought for a few moments, 'yes, yes, in a way, I suppose I do. Let me try to explain.'

'Time,' he began, gesturing for me to take the chair facing his, across the big, functional steel desk, empty but for a framed picture of his wife, 'is not as most people imagine it, a single strip, unrolling from past to future, in a continuous day-at-a-time fashion. It's more like a thick stew, with all the elements co-mingling.'

'All the elements?' I interrupted, already baffled.

'Yes, time isn't a series of linear events, it's one great mix of everything that has ever been. Yesterday still there alongside today, pre-history flowing along next to the twenty-first century.'

'But surely, things do occur in sequence. Doesn't what happens on Tuesday depend on what happened on Monday? You know, cause and effect?'

'There's no such phenomenon! You think that if you don't throw the ball you can't break the window, but I'm saying that if the window is already broken, then the ball has to be thrown. Time is a single construct; there's no past or present, only existence, you see?'

'No! I don't...and where does Bryony come into all this?'

He sighed, 'What our research was telling us, hers and mine, is that under certain circumstances it can be possible to glimpse those other moments in existence, stir two parts of the mix together, to return to the stew analogy.'

'Our piece of carrot bumping up against yesterday's dumpling?' I suggested, in an attempt to lighten the mood.

'In a way, but you have to forget about the concept of "yesterday" and think of it as another "now".

'Easy enough for you to say,' I countered, 'but carry on, please.'

'Ghosts manifest themselves on those occasions when such interactions come about spontaneously. When two component parts of what we call time, briefly fuse and overlap - like a double exposure on a film-strip. It's likely that if you spot a ghost, the ghost is spotting you in exactly the same way - and probably with the same trepidation. You're both totally alive in your own "now".

'You mean that if I saw the ghost of a Roman legionary, he'd be seeing the ghost of a research facility employee. He in my past - no, not the past, just another part of time - and visa versa.'

'Now you've got it.'

'And Bryony?'

'I found a way to "encourage" that overlap. Just for a few minutes. It's the last time she was in the laboratory and each evening we meet, and share that piece of time.'

'As ghosts.'

'If you mean that we are somewhat insubstantial, yes, but we are aware of each other, we can communicate.'

'And does she know that she will die?'

'She won't! You are forgetting already that she lives in a fragment of time that she will always occupy. Her death occurs elsewhere, and always will.'

'And how long are your meetings?'

'A little under ten minutes - but it's enough! Enough for us to remember - everything.'

Fifty Percent of Infinity

'But look,' I frowned again, trying to hold onto the thought that had formed in my mind, 'you visit her in her particular moment of time, one in which she is unchanging - she must be, she can't age if it's the same moment,' I faltered in my exposition, the concept slipping away, 'but you, you are aging. Each night at eight o' four you are another day older, aren't you?'

'I am,' replied my friend, sadly, and he turned his face away and wiped at his eyes. 'The overlap could only be performed once. We could only meet once more but that meeting will last forever. It's a part of the stew now, he and she will share the same ten minutes of time until eternity.'

'But the whole of your lives together is a part of the stew,' I protested, 'and it's of no consolation to you here, now. How can those ten minutes matter?'

'They matter because I regain what I had lost,' he said, 'Bryony has been dead and she lives again. She understands my anguish, comforts me in my misery.'

'But you're only playing with time,' I retorted, 'pulling the puzzle apart and re-arranging the pieces in a different order.

'At last, you understand,' said my friend, taking the photograph from the desk and placing it, face downwards into a drawer.

World's End

On Monday Michael waited for the world to end; on Tuesday he went shopping for beans.

So, has it all been a lie? he asked himself, as he stood back allowing a tall man with an angry face, room to join the checkout queue ahead of him. He wasn't good with figures, and dates were figures too, weren't they, so maybe he had become confused, despite all of Pieter's instructions. Then he saw the supermarket clock, confirming the day and the date and he knew that Tansy had been right after all.

***

They'd first met in The Homeless Child, one evening when Michael had called in to see Tansy, who worked there, behind the bar. She wasn't a proper girlfriend, they didn't go out together, or meet outside the pub but she was kind to him and sometimes, when the gang from the estate were getting noisy and calling him names, she would shout at them to leave him alone, and smile the kindest smile he had ever seen, just for him.

It was on one of those occasions that Pieter had appeared, taken his arm and guided him to a table; had bought him a cider and invited him to share the greatest secret of all time.

He was dark, Pieter, with a sharp beard and a trace of accent that might have come from any one of a dozen places and, like Tansy, when he smiled the smile opened Michael's heart. And Tansy, Michael noted, not without some satisfaction, was a little jealous of his new friendship, because when they were together, as they were with increasing frequency, he sometimes caught sight of her looking their way, and marring her pretty face with a frown.

It was because of her concern that he made sure she was busy elsewhere whenever he passed Pieter the money his friend reluctantly requested of him: money that would enable preparations for the final day, to continue.

And Michael had money, his mother's solicitor had explained this to him carefully after her death. A sum paid into his account each month, with more, should he show a future need. He had told Pieter of the arrangement, in a bid to lessen the other's obvious feelings of concern at accepting his gifts, and, in return, Pieter had told him when the world would end.

Of course, Pieter had not shared his secret knowledge straight away. He had spoken only of important research, something vital to both their futures. He told Michael that the details of his quest were too complicated to share, that he must bear responsibility alone, and Michael, excited to find himself a party to such events, played the only part allowed him.

They had met at Easter and when Christmas was nearly upon them, Pieter, perhaps unable to withstand Michael's constant demands for more information, had finally divulged the findings of his work: at midnight, on Sunday, December twenty-first, the world would cease to be.

Michael was understandably shocked and then scared by the revelation. Why? he wanted to know. How? But Pieter was not forthcoming on either the reasons for the planet's demise or the method to be employed. As to Michael's next question, was there nothing they could do to stop it? that he pondered for some time, before giving his answer.

Maybe there was, he replied at last. Maybe, if they could raise the funds, he could invoke the necessary intervention. More money, a little more money, might just save them both. Then he gave Michael a sideways look, as if he was unsure of his friend's response and Michael, his heart racing, said that yes, he could get the money, he would visit his solicitor and explain everything and...

And Pieter had interrupted and told him to slow down, that he, Pieter could not save everyone, and they should think this through and that perhaps if he told the man who dealt with his mother's money that he needed the finance for a holiday that might be better for all concerned.

Michael had nodded to this and the very next morning had called at his solicitor's offices but the interview had not gone well.

The man behind the desk had asked where Michael was going and how soon he would be leaving and Michael, having given no thought to these matters, stuttered into silence and then sat through a stern instruction on the correct use of his inheritance and the importance of thinking through his plans properly. After that the man's tone became kindlier and he asked if he might help in the making of the arrangements, but by then Michael, red-faced and near tears, wanted only to be free of the place and fled to The Homeless Child to seek the solace of Tansy's smile.

It was mid-morning and the bar was deserted as he poured out the story, his grief multiplying as he realised that he was acquainting Tansy with her own death.

When he had finished, she regarded him with the saddest expression he had ever seen, before walking to the door and dropping the catch and then ushering him to one of the upholstered corner benches and taking a chair to face him across the table.

She did not look frightened at the news he had given her, in fact, when she spoke, he realised her mood was more one of growing anger.

Michael, Michael, it was all a trick, she had cried, a daft story to dupe him out of the cash his mother had left for his care. The world wasn't about to end! Pieter was a crook, a conman, a fraudster, a lowlife; scum of the worst sort, who'd pray on the vulnerable without a second thought for the consequences. Michael had tried to tell her she was wrong, but she wouldn't listen. Next time he sets foot in this bar I'll call the police she had promised, before walking him to the door and, having sought his assurance that he would be all right, had released him from her sanctuary with a kiss on the cheek that had fortified him for the rest of that day and through till midnight, when he waited with growing anxiety for the crack of doom and felt nothing but emptiness when the mantle clock ticked on regardless.

And so, he was here, later that same morning, buying beans and bread and watching life flow on around him.

He was still in a state of introspection when he finally reached the checkout and looked up to see a familiar figure manning the till point.

In a blue overall and matching tie Pieter did not immediately register as the man who had gained his trust and left him disillusioned. When he did realise who sat before him, all the pent-up rage and frustration from a sleepless, angst-filled night boiled over and he hurled the can of beans at the cause of his distress and followed up with his fists as Pieter stood and tried to make his escape from the confines of the check-out. When he did free himself, backing away to the staff-room door, Michael pursued him, grabbing items from waiting trolleys and hurling them after.

World's End

Then they were both through the door and Pieter was turning, grabbing his pursuer by the arms and wrestling him to the ground where Michael lay, his anger spent, his breath coming in great sobs of emotion.

"You...bastard!" It was the worst curse Michael knew and he voiced it with all the venom he could command. "You, bloody, bloody, bastard!"

Then Pieter was down beside him, a comforting hand on his shoulder, a look of concern on his face.

"Michael, Michael," he said, repeating the name in an odd echo of Tansy's remonstrations on the previous day, "what is it mate? What's the problem? It all turned out OK in the end, didn't it?"

Michael looked up into the familiar face and scrubbed away his tears. "Alright?" he said, "alright? When everything you ever told me was a lie? That the world would end, that we could be saved - if I could just get the money, except I couldn't, could I? and it didn't matter, cos it didn't happen and we're still here. All bloody lies."

Pieter looked back at him, his face unreadable. "Come on Michael, you know you can trust me," he said at last, adding, "it was never about the money, you know that. I told you that the world would end and that we could be saved," he paused and his gaze intensified, "and Michael, it did end and we were...saved! No big bang. One existence just faded away, and we moved to another. A new world, just like the old but with lots of exciting new possibilities - you'll see!"

Michael stared up, his mind racing and then, as he saw how it might be so, he lay back and returned the smile that had spread across Pieter's face.

Fifty Percent of Infinity

Information Overload

Author's note: only some of the information expounded in this story is true - it is up to the reader to determine which that might be.

Brian hadn't always been addicted to information retrieval. There had been a time, before the competition, when he'd been happy to learn no more than he was told by his daily newspaper - even though he was vaguely aware that the tabloid in question had its own agenda. Never the less, the opinions and attitudes which he saw expressed there seemed to mirror his own view of the world and he found its brash and irreverent approach to life curiously informative.

In this way, he had become quite certain about a number of things: that any event, however momentous, could be announced in words of no more than four letters; that, when following the letter "F", the asterisk was the most useful punctuation mark in the journalist's lexicon; and that any red-blooded male's career of choice was photographer of the girls who displayed their attributes on page three.

In view of the latter, it was especially appropriate that it should be one of these who became responsible for an unexpected expansion in Brian's world-view.

The technology revolution had passed him by, leaving him owning no electronic gadget more sophisticated than an electric toothbrush, indeed the only reason his attention had been drawn to the competition at all had

Fifty Percent of Infinity

been the young lady cradling the prize to her ample and overexposed bosom. On closer examination - both of the bosom and the competition - it had struck Brian that choosing the correct answer to the question: is the capital of England, a) Ulan Bator, b) London or c) Phnom Penh, was simplified by the fact that he had previously heard of one of the possible answers. With this advantage over his fellow readers it came as no surprise when he was judged the winner and became the owner of a state-of-the-art computer system.

Having exhausted his limited knowledge of such equipment by plugging the labelled items together and switching on the mains current, Brian called for assistance in the rather rotund shape of his friend and confidant, Milo Tusker. Milo held court at the saloon bar of The Legless Ferret and would, for a fee, sort out those problems that inevitably come the way of the computer illiterate in possession of a computer. Having crossed Milo's palm with the requisite pint of Old Particular, Brian soon found himself immersed in the world of the Internet.

His first forays were tentative and found him merely transferring his reading habit to the online version of his favourite paper, but all that changed when one morning he dropped his electric razor into the hand-basin. The razor was plugged in for recharging and reacted badly to immersion in soapy water and Brian put its replacement at the top of his "to do" list. Over breakfast, as he gave consideration to the best local electrical retailers, the thought suddenly came to him that, with his newly acquired skills in IT, he might "surf the net" and "buy online".

Sitting tremulously at his keyboard, he typed the words "electric razor" into the search engine's window and hit return. Almost at once a page of entries appeared on screen and Brian selected one, at random,

Information Overload

double-clicked his mouse and peered attentively at the monitor.

The article that revealed itself was not what he had expected. "Electric razors - electromagnetic wave source and its link to brain tumours" read the abbreviated summary. Brian leaned forward and began to read.

A dozen triple-bladed safety razors and a can of foam cost considerably less than even the cheapest electric shaver and, as Brian made his way home later that afternoon, he congratulated himself on saving not only his life but a good many pounds sterling into the bargain.

And the incident got him thinking: did all questions asked of the worldwide web receive multiple answers? He tried the name of the pot plant on his windowsill and was staggered to be presented, in 0.48 seconds, with 36,150,226 linked references. Among only the first dozen he found not merely details of the plant and its cultivation but a cure for alopecia prepared from its leaves and a heavy metal band named after the condition. Brian looked them up and discovered that their drummer was a direct descendant of the first person to be run over by a steam charabanc in the state of Nevada, which vehicle had, several years later, a further search told him, blown its boiler and destroyed a bridge across the Navanada River, a water course formed by two millennia of erosion, which had revealed the only known fossil of a double-tailed fish from the Cretaceous. He clicked on. The fish was named after a nineteenth-century opera star who came from the small Italian hill town of Montefianni, famous as the location of French film director Jean Claude Nontand's epic, La Guêpe de l'Été est Mort (The Summer Wasp is Dead). The English cinematographer on this movie came from Frinton, a town famous for a campaign in 2009 to save the old-style level-crossing gates, which Network Rail never the less subsequently replaced with continental-type lifting barriers. And the history of Network Rail proved to be fascinating too, with surprising links to Genghis Khan's daughter-in-law and a calico undergarment worn by Cossack tribesmen.

Brian looked up and saw that it was a quarter-past one in the morning.

***

'Eh? Oh eh!' The strange sound was Milo acknowledging Brian's concerns whilst downing a full tankard of best bitter in one swallow. 'Yeah, ahhh!' he wiped his sleeve across his beard, nudged the vessel across the table and broke wind enthusiastically. 'That's the whole point o' the net. Ent it? The whole world joined up in one glorious brew! Look, don't you hold back, me old charmer! Fill yer boots, so t' speak.'

And Brian couldn't hold back. An enquiry for the opening times of the local market garden prompted investigation of an article on Bolivian parrots, which, in turn, led to an essay on tropical diseases, a video of Dutch Dyke Pole Vaulting and medieval chutney recipes. By the time he nodded off at his desk, he'd additionally explored initiation ceremonies for Iberian stonemasons, the life cycle of parasitic liver worms and the under-lying principles of ten-dimensional string theory. By the end of that week he was hugely more informed on a hundred esoteric subjects but already beginning to lose touch with events in his immediate vicinity.

He found out about Mavis whilst searching for the history of homoerotic arm-wrestling. His quest had led him rather unexpectedly to a social networking site where a familiar name caught his eye and further investigation disclosed that his long-time girlfriend was on holiday in Tossa De Mar - with Milo Tusker! And

Information Overload

there were alarming references to a story in the tabloids.

Brian hadn't even glanced at his old newspaper for weeks. He hadn't cancelled the delivery because it came in useful as somewhere to stand the cat's dish but since his conversion to the global information pool he had come to think of it as sordid and one dimensional. Still, rather than follow up the story online, he trotted into the kitchen, brushed the dried Comficat morsels into the bin and stared at the front page in fascination.

Below the headline, NERD WINS MEGA CASH WITH PC PROG!! there was a photograph of a beach-front scene in which Mavis hugged a now clean-shaven Milo, he attired in an alarming paisley-print mankini and making a gesture for which the paper had provided a careful if redundant translation utilising an "F" and a smattering of asterisks.

Brian carried the paper back to his desk and read through the story. Milo had worked out a foolproof formula for winning at blackjack and had amassed a fortune at the resort's casino before being banned from every gambling joint this side of McMurdo Sound. His expletive-enhanced pronouncements had been aimed at the casino's owners but Brian couldn't help but take them as personal ridicule.

He frowned. Could it be that, after all, it was the tabloid that had its finger on the pulse of the real world and the rest was simply garbage - intriguing but ultimately useless background chatter? As he brooded on the photograph his eye wandered to the hilltop castle beyond the beach and his fingers idly keyed the name of the location and tapped at the return.

***

The battlements were fourteenth century and the artist Marc Chagall had lived below them after the

Fifty Percent of Infinity

Second World War. Chagall had been commissioned to paint the ceiling of the Paris opera, the director of which, in 1780 had been one Francois Joseph Gossec, composer of a popular gavotte that, centuries later, was borrowed by a husband of film star Betty Hutton and used extensively as incidental music in Warner Brothers Looney Tunes cartoons.

As Brian typed "Looney Tunes" into the search panel the newspaper slipped down amongst the cobwebbed cables behind the monitor, leaving only Milo's eyes regarding him derisively over the edge of the desk.

Unquiet Meals

'Cream tangerine, Howard? Ginger sling with a pineapple heart? Pop a protein pill and put your armour on! Enterprising crewmen used to rustle up a rib eye just by punching in the permutations. You and me babe? We make do with standard issue pap, Pappy! Pour us a nice red, something from the north side of the vineyard, with just a hint of salamander. Only the virtuous shall have no cakes and ale, and we, Howard, have very little virtuosity, that's our downfall. Downfall, fall down, fal de diddle dey do! You can learn a lot about a man over a good plate of pasta; pass de Parmesan if you please! I feel a song coming on - but first, the repast, that's my riposte! Did you know that onions only make you cry on weekdays?'

'Mr Lanchester, the medi-pod contains a comprehensive range of treatments for all forms of psychosis, I really do feel you would benefit from its ministrations...'

Accident log: Service Shuttle Aldebaran: 40:75:58 Standard.

Here are the basic facts as I see them. At around 1200hrs ship time, the cargo vessel 'Lightning Reaction' emerged from N space to carry out routine procedures and was struck by debris from an unknown source, sustaining damage to the QP Drive that led, in turn, to an explosion and the total destruction of said vessel. The Service Shuttle Aldebaran was conducting a trans-ship manoeuvre at

Fifty Percent of Infinity

the time of impact and was thrown clear of the subsequent explosion. On board Flight Engineer Howard Rockwell and Passenger Dominic Lanchester. Automated systems corrected the imparted spin and brought The Aldebaran back under control of the AI within one standard time unit.

'You know, Howard, there was a time when cabbages were kings. Artichokes were the New Jerusalem. Capercaillie counted for something back then; stuffed with a nice bit of thyme and sage but only if you had the time. That was a joke, Howard. I like a good joke. Do you remember Alfred Limber? No? Great comedian; played that nightclub they hollowed out on Deimos. I was there when he had his seizure. Not if I sees ya first! Oh, he was so...can you feel a draught in here? I thought I could feel a draught. I don't suppose you could have left the airlock open, just a fraction? No, I suppose not.'

'I've noticed, Mr Lanchester, that you no longer complete the daily log and I'm sure that doing so has considerable therapeutic value.'

'A draught of cold, strong beer would do us both a world of good, don't you think, Howard? Invigorate the cardiovascular system, send those old corpuscles racing. You have a tendency towards corpulence, if you don't mind my mentioning it. Corpulent corpuscles do no good for man nor beast. Slim is the word. Slim pickings, Slim Whitman - he was a singer you know, twentieth century, that's my field, I majored in it at Olympus Mons. Ask me a question, go on. Any question. Oh, Rosemarie, I love you. You don't mind if I call you Rose? It was my mother's favourite soap. There's another joke there, but I won't bother, my erudition's lost on you. Fancy a Garibaldi?

Unquiet Meals

The AI says I should complete this report daily but I'm pretty sure it's only trying to occupy my time. Thing is, I should be dead, well, I should be alive - and back on Mars. See, I was only aboard the Lightning Reaction because of Russell.

"I've won transit to Cygnus Forty" he said, "and I can't go, you can see that, what with Caramel and all, so I thought - Dom, he'd love to see The Brittle Mountains and The Sea of Path, and it's not as if you're doing anything, is it?"

I let that last bit pass; I've got my reasons for remaining solo, and I thought, why not, and that's how I came to be a passenger on the LR. It wasn't exactly luxury travel but what can you expect from a competition in the Phobos Observer?

So, I should have died with the rest of those poor sods but then Howard invited me to take a spin in the shuttle.

"We're taking advantage of breaking out of N space,' he told me, 'to shift a few of the empty cargo cubes. It'll make things easier later on at Cygnus."

Because the Lightning never entered atmosphere there was no need to contain its cargo in any way. The storage cubes were just stacked neatly, in a holding area within the ship's open superstructure.

As luck would have it we were locked tight to a cube when the debris-field hit. The containment cage was ripped from its housing and the shuttle did a head over heels out into space. When the Lightning blew we were spinning too hard to see what went on and, by the time everything calmed down, there was just us and a patch of hot, glowing dust which we were leaving astern as the AI set course for the nearest inhabited world.

'A mild sedation would ease the tedium of the journey, Mr Lanchester.'

Fifty Percent of Infinity

'Far and few, far and few, Howard, are the lands were the Jumblies can provide us with bed and board. As you've told me often enough, there ain't no cryogenics on this here craft so we're here for the duration and you need someone to share the watch.'

'Mr Lanchester, please consider: since we have been unable to jettison the cube, the nearest space port, Jowett's Funnel, is fifteen point three years distant at the shuttle's current velocity. We are five years into the journey and as anticipated, the recyclers are providing the necessary supplies of oxygen and food but we lack distractions to keep the mind occupied, Mr Lanchester.'

'Hold off! unhand me, grey-beard loon! You triangulated our position and set us on course for the new world my friend, and I remain eternally grateful for your valiant efforts, but I cannot submit to your request to accept the embrace of Morpheus. Navigationally speaking, Howard, your OK but your fears for my sanity are unfounded. Now, spring to the stirrup and into the midnight we'll gallop abreast! There's much to be done and little time in which to skin the rabbit. Cry, chocks away and let slip the dogs of war.'

The AI says that in the absence of an unlikely rescue, we must spend a decade and a half on this tiny craft. I'm relatively young and physically I can outlive the transit but mentally the prospect terrifies me. The shuttle is a utilitarian device designed for brief sorties; there are no books, no music, no film. Already I suspect that before we sight land I will have wrenched open that enticing double-door and committed myself to the deeps of space.

Meanwhile I occupy myself with thoughts of food. We have the processor and more than a sufficiency of powdered compounds with which to prepare our

Unquiet Meals

meals but the fare is bland and at night fantasies of gargantuan banquets fill my dreams.

'Engastration; do you know what that is, Howard? The Tudors used to stuff a turkey with a goose stuffed with a chicken and the chicken itself was stuffed with a partridge stuffed, in its turn, with a pigeon. It hardly seems enough, do you think? I slaver at the prospect of an outer emu, then an ostrich - they are avians of Old Earth, Howard - what a shame it is that aepyornis maximus is no longer extant. The elephant bird, Howard, a creature you could really get your teeth into! Oh, bring me some figgy pudding and a fine custard, for we can't forget dessert.'

Oh, dear God! a decade still remains of this interminable flight. I sleep badly and wake curiously content for the time it takes me to recall our plight, then feelings of despair engulf me again and I fight them, fight them, fight them and each time they gain a little ground and I seek sleep and its escape and I fear the night for the realisation the morning will bring.

'Why, Howard, are you so insistent regarding our diet? I know the tubes and packets meet our needs nutritionally but there's more to eating than mere ingestion. The cube's refrigerated and the access port's undogged. There's red meat still within that hold; what say a tenderloin tonight?'

'Mr Lanchester, forgive me when I say that much of what you believe is delusional; understandably so, but you would not give such matters consideration if you were in your right mind. I repeat: a course of the appropriate medication could restore you to a proper equilibrium.'

'Oh hum, Howard, not that old nostrum. Half a pound of tuppeny rice, a penny for my thoughts.

Fifty Percent of Infinity

Dinner's planned and the invitations sent. Break out the best linen and the Sunday silver, for we shall have feasting in the great hall and tomorrow I wed.'

I let go and fall and the void swallows me up and there will be a reckoning but I have no care for that, if I can touch the livid form within the darkness and sate my hunger on its tender flesh.

'Mr Lanchester, can you see what you have done? A report will have to be filed.'

'A report, Howard? For enjoying a good meal? Tell them that, for once, the prisoner ate a hearty supper. A bloody steak and a glass of red. And we shall dine again, you and I, for the carcass is sufficient; but we will ration it and prolong our pleasure. We've a long journey ahead, Howard, but the hold is cold.'

'Mr Lanchester, I am not Howard Rockwell, I am the AI in control of this shuttle. Howard Rockwell died when The Aldebaran spun clear of the Lightning Response. We stored his body in the refrigerated hold of the cube for repatriation on arrival at Jowett's Funnel. Please try to remember.'

'But I do remember, Howard, I do. We stab it with our steely knives, Howard, and although I try to be strong, the flesh is weak; the flesh is weak.'

Printed in Great Britain
by Amazon